Best Vegan Science Fiction & Fiction & Fantasy

2019

Also from Metaphorosis

<u>Verdage</u>

Reading 5X5 x2: Duets
Score – an SFF symphony
Reading 5X5: Readers' Edition
Reading 5X5: Writers' Edition

<u>Metaphorosis Magazine</u>

Metaphorosis: Best of 20xx
Metaphorosis 20xx: The Complete Stories
annual issues, from 2016

Monthly issues

<u>Plant Based Press</u>

Best Vegan Science Fiction & Fantasy
annual issues, from 2016

from B. Morris Allen:
Susurrus
Allenthology: Volume I
Tocsin: and other stories
Start with Stones: collected stories
Metaphorosis: a collection of stories

Best Vegan Science Fiction & Fantasy

2019

edited by
B. Morris Allen

ISBN: 978-1-64076-005-9 (e-book)
ISBN: 978-1-64076-006-6 (paperback)

from
Metaphorosis Publishing

Neskowin

Contents

Copyright

Metaphorosis Publishing

From the Editor

When I was looking forward to this anthology in late 2019, neither I nor anyone else anticipated the situation we find ourselves in now. Even when I finished selecting stories in early March 2020, most didn't realize the magnitude of what was happening with COVID-19. As it spread, we learned something about what our leaders are made of, and a lot of it isn't good.

We also learned something about our neighbours, though, and some of that is good. There are people who don't think twice about the effect they may have on others, and there are those who are very careful. There are those who ignore risk by urging dangerous action, and those who ignore risk because they have to – because it's their job to save lives or because it's their job to sell essential products face to face.

No one's been perfect in facing this situation. I know I've made compromises I don't feel proud of. But most of us are trying, at least – to make ourselves and our loved ones safer, and to make the world better in some way.

Obviously, this is also a crisis that didn't just *happen* to us, but I'm not going to go into the factors that helped bring it and its siblings on – the factory farms, the wet markets, etc. The point of these anthologies is to imagine better – a world where we *have* learned better, where life isn't quite as cruel.

Not all the stories in this anthology are happy ones, but a number of them are. And one thing that most of them share is a theme of growth and learning. Sometimes it's hard or painful. Sometimes it means breaking down your idols and traditions and setting new goals. But most of the time, it's for the better. Not always, because life doesn't work that way. But even when life doesn't go as planned, we can still learn something.

That's the theme of this anthology, then, in this time of hardship and crisis – dream of something better; and when reality doesn't measure up, go try to fix it, in whatever way you can.

B. Morris Allen
Editor
1 May 2020

The Lonely King

Gunnar De Winter

Once, he'd had loyal subjects.

Now he only had bricks and sand.

Immortality was not a blessing.

He had dragged his throne to the highest tower of town. It had been an arduous task, but he'd had – quite literally – all the time in the world.

The top of the tower had long since crumbled, exposing king and throne alike to the elements. Mocking desert winds threw hails of sand at the king's weathered face. He clutched a parchment in his lap, a letter from a love long lost, but that too became taunting sand. The king squinted but stubbornly refused to yield to the desert.

Everything blurred to yellow. Fierce, burning yellow. Even the decrepit town buildings had taken on the color of the desert that surrounded them.

Then, a change.

This is it, thought the king. *Madness has finally found me.*

His kingdom, after all, was devoid of humanity. He was all that was left.

And yet, the flicker on the horizon persisted. Multiplied.

The king blinked rapidly, thinking grains of sand stuck to the surface of his eyes.

But the distant dots continued to come closer. They could have been animals, hunting for rare prey. No, the specks were too... intent, too strongly aimed at him.

He maintained his composure even though his heart almost leapt out of his chest. The dots were human – unmistakable now. A few dozen. Even beasts of burden trundled alongside. Druks, judging by the typical swaying gait of the massive brawny hexapods.

Their goal was clear now. They were headed straight for him.

Alone no longer.

Let my reign find breath again.

The king's joints creaked into activity after eons of statuesque silence. He descended two steps at a time. How his mother would have chided him. Such expression of haste was not royal. There was no such thing as imperial impatience, she always said.

But there was no one to witness the childish giddiness of an ancient monarch. Not yet, anyway.

One half of the town's large wooden gate was rusted shut, a giant rooted in the dry earth. The other half barely held on, another giant, one that hovered over an abyss with only a fraying rope to clutch at.

The king stood waiting in the triangular opening that remained. His heavy coat had left a wide trail through the sand that covered every bare surface in the town.

"Welcome," he bellowed when he thought his new subjects were within earshot.

They stopped and looked at each other. Surprised. Uncomfortable. As if they weren't expecting the king to welcome them.

Nonsense, the king thought. *A good ruler acknowledges his subjects. If they do not know this, they were right to flee their faltering sovereign.*

Following a huddle amongst the travelers, the caravan set in motion again.

Then king felt a broad grin appear within the crags of his weathered face.

The leader of the caravan was a tall man – certainly for a mortal. A full head shorter than the king, he came to a halt a few paces away. His eyes couldn't meet those of his new monarch. He rubbed the back of his head, messing up his thick brown locks.

"Uhm... we didn't expect to..."

The king swung his arm. "Leave it be, good man. Say no more. You are all welcome here." He looked down on his new loyal follower and put a hand on the man's shoulder. Muscles tensed under the king's touch. *Nervous, no doubt.*

"Together, we shall rebuild this kingdom."

That night, the thrill of once again ruling more than an empire of solitude spurred the king's rusted memory. He remembered...

The king remembered a time when the desert was dappled with small king- and queendoms, when immortal houses of rulers formed a robust tree of genealogical ties. Each adult immortal had its town of subjects, but kings and queens frequently visited each other. Squabbles were few and the lives of kings and subjects alike were – generally – good. The desert and its creatures were always a looming threat, but the kingdoms were oases of civilization. The king relished the memory. It had been a time of happiness, even of love. Once, he had had a queen.

Then, one day, those lights of culture faded one by one, in the blink of an immortal's eye. Kings and queens increasingly yielded to the desert, leaving their subordinates helpless. Kingdoms crumbled, eagerly swallowed by the encroaching sea of sand. The rulers that remained turned in on themselves, protecting their own above all else. So too did the king. Contact dwindled. Isolation flourished.

There were no more visits.

A true king intervenes as little as possible.

He let them settle in at their own pace, let them find their own place. After all, except for his tower, all buildings were available for use and occupation.

The morning came with new sounds. The grating creaks of rusted hinges, the crunch of sand under boots. The wail of a child.

And was that...? Yes, the smell of freshly baked bread. The king's withered salivary glands refilled, rejoiced. Though monarchs didn't require sustenance, they appreciated complex flavors.

Patience.

For the first weeks, the king simply watched them from his tower. They seemed like ants scurrying under his gaze. When you were outside time, time became malleable. The king's excitement, though, was immortal. Atemporal.

His new flock had established itself and had begun rebuilding the town. Hinges stopped creaking, sand was swept out of buildings and compacted into avenues. A productive lot.

They would need guidance. And he would be their guide. As he was meant to be.

He walked down the stairs for the second time since the new arrivals had entered his realm. Slowly now, regal.

Sand no longer screeched beneath his sandals as he strode across the cleaned streets, a sound he was glad to miss. There was another sound, though, that died as he emerged from his tower. A sound he did miss.

The sound of laughter, of conversation, of life.

The people were still apprehensive.

But I have given them time. Oh, how their previous monarch must have been monstrous. My task is larger than I thought. I shall not waver.

He smiled, ancient creases in his face performing movements they were still unused to.

"Good day!" His voice rang across town. The people cowered.

Enthusiasm can be frightening for those that are not enthused, he reminded himself. *Slowly. Even the timeless can go too fast.*

He took a deep breath. The air was cleaner, full of aromatics. The taste, the smell of everyday activity, of habitation, soothed him.

"I am pleased," he said – softer now. "You have made tremendous progress. This place," he swept a long, emaciated arm, "has not looked this good, this vibrant since... a very long time." *Ward off the sadness, it is not their burden.*

The caravan's leader – unofficial mayor now – frowned with worry as his kinsmen slowly retreated, eyes averted from the king in their midst.

Poor things. How they must have suffered.

"Tell me, good man," the king spoke softly, containing the royal strength in his voice, "what is your name?"

The man swallowed and sighed. "I am Bramm."

"Bramm." The king stepped closer but halted as soon as he saw the muscles in Bramm's arms tense like cables being pulled too hard. "I am no fool. Tell me what worries you."

Bramm's cheeks clenched so hard the king feared his teeth might shatter.

"Fear not, you are safe here. Speak freely."

Another sigh. "We... Our town was ruined by our monarch. He was... not right. So, we fled, looking for a place to be free."

"A wise choice."

"A place without king or queen."

The thought struck the king like a punch to the gut. He stepped back unwillingly. *Heresy!* Rage bubbled. *No. Control. Restraint. Do not lash out. Their trauma is not their own creation.*

"I see." The king closed his eyes and took another deep breath. *Life, joy, the air is full of it. Do not squander it.* "I can assure you that your tribulations are over. Not only will you be safe here, together we will make this place a thriving community where all can flourish."

Why do they not cheer, why do they not revel in their newfound peace?

Bramm mumbled something, the meaning lost in the song of wind and sand.

"What was that, my friend?"

"But we would not be free."

"I... You are mistaken, Bramm. But I understand. You need time to heal from oppression. I can give you time." The king turned a deaf ear to Bramm's mumbling and blind eyes to the man's shaking head. The immortal headed back to his tower. *Free? How can they be free without ruler, without rules?*

The royal mind was in turmoil. Heaving emotions threw up another memory from eons past.

The king recalled one of his mentors, a king among kings, an immortal ruler that had been around when consciousness congealed out of the mists of the universe. As was custom, visiting monarchs often spent time with those in training.

Those with the most thriving, resilient kingdoms preached patience as the main virtue of a good ruler. The king-to-be spent many nights ruminating on his mentors' teachings about the idiosyncratic minds of the ephemerals, the differences that separated rulers from their subjects, and how a true king embraced this gap for the betterment of all.

Days passed in a fever dream as the king's thoughts went back and forth in an endless pursuit of each other. A pursuit without victor. There was conflict inside the king. What he wanted was right there, yet out of reach. *If you can't rule their hearts, your kingdom is empty.*

From his tower, the king saw Bramm hug his wife and ruffle his son's hair. They were laughing, looking longingly at each other. Complete.

There was love, family among his subjects.

Perhaps a queen could remedy the loneliness. Bah, banish the thought. There was only one queen for me, and she is no more.

Now, his subjects were his children, his recalcitrant lovers, his purpose.

Still...

His subconscious violently pulled him out of his reverie.

Something was amiss.

There.

On the horizon something moved. Aggressively, with predatory purpose. Only one thing could move like that. Sandpards, with six strong legs and a muscular body to support a large triangular head that was more jaw than brain.

The king sprang from his chair, ready to warn his people.

Wait. Not yet. Within the blink of an eye, he stopped moving and turned still as a sculpture. *This will teach them they need me. When they see the value of my presence, they will have no other option but to come to me for protection.*

Sandpards always moved in sixes. They were fast. Very fast.

The king chewed his bottom lip. *Come on, misguided mortals, you must see now that you need me.*

Shouts washed towards him like salve being applied to a fresh wound. His elation grew with the panic below.

Any second now, they will run up the stairs, to me.

But no, they ran outwards, towards the feeble cracked ramparts they had not yet completely fixed.

Fools.

A sandpard could scale those easily. A king knew these things. After all, kings and beasts were made from the same sand.

His flock was in danger.

The king roared and jumped from his tower. He called on the power of the sand to guide his descent. Every grain in the town sang to him, danced for him. A small tornado cushioned his feet and lessened the impact on his joints as he landed. He shot forward.

Slow. Too slow. Rest rusts.

Backed by a wave of sand, he reached the edge of town, where two sandpards had already leapt across the barricades. He struck one beast with his scepter. The other one bit his free arm, nearly swallowing half of it. The king looked at the creature and growled.

"I am the sand, I am the desert." The king's arm turned to sand. The sandpard wheezed until its triple double-lobed lungs were saturated. The beast suffocated and collapsed.

The king fell to his knees, unaware of the shocked silence around him. Then came the scream.

The sandpard matriarch had found a victim. The king surged to his feet and pulled his newly forming arm out of the sand. His new limb was still coalescing when he saw Bramm lunge at the sandpard. The man's son lay limp beneath the beast's hungry jaws.

Brave but foolish.

The king knocked Bramm aside as the sandpard leapt. Beast and king locked in a lethal embrace, a deathly dance within a whirlwind. The inertia of eternity became the flash of violence. Sand settled. Royalty and savagery stared at each other, panting. The sandpard mewled. Its smooth skin granulated, cracked. Beast became sand. It crumbled and collapsed.

Sandpards weren't clever, except when it came to hunting. The three remaining sandpards, about to finish the circling movement that would bring them to the other side of town, lost heart. With the matriarch out of the picture, they howled and ran off.

The king straightened and rubbed the sand from his sweaty face.

Now they will understand they need me.

"You demon!" Bramm came towards him, his eyes boring into the king's face for the first time. Anger and grief reddened his face and streaked his cheeks with tears. "We do not want you here. We never wanted you here. My son..." Bramm's voice cracked. "You couldn't even save my son," he continued softly, sinking to his knees. "You can't protect us. You... you are nothing. Go. Just go."

The king's chest heaved. *But I waited for your love, your respect. You want protection without rule? You want the protection of a king without accepting his rule?*

The eternal being bellowed. "You ungrateful bastards! Without me, you would have all perished." The town trembled as the sand shifted. "There can be no kingdom without king. We monarchs are life, we are guardians. Without us the desert would swallow you all." The wind wailed along with him.

The fear in the people's eyes stabbed the king's old heart. Anger and wind subsided in tandem.

As befit a king, he strategically redeployed to his sanctuary.

Suppressed anger and a wounded heart birthed another memory from the sands of time.

The king remembered a queen. A queen many ages his senior, but as striking as any immortal could aspire to be. A well of knowledge that only few possessed. As young king and new ruler of his own small kingdom, he often went to visit her. In his dreams, he already saw their children building a new network of prosperous kingdoms.

The king remembered the first night they had lain together. After the throes of passion had ebbed away, the queen whispered stories to him about the birth of the immortals, myths of how the earth itself – the one true parent of the immortals – had begotten them to keep the desert from spreading over the entirety of the world. The desert, so the queen told her devoted listener, was a cancer, always looking to spread and consume. The immortals were scattered across it to stunt its growth, to provide a counterweight and establish balance. The king and his kin accepted this duty and made it their purpose.

They would not dare!

Bramm's rage had lit a fire in the townspeople. They knew they couldn't best a monarch. But they also knew that without kingdom, kings perished. A monarch would never – could never – leave his town except for a visit to another monarch. His people, though, could travel as they pleased.

Will they really choose the cancerous desert over me? Am I so terrible? Do they truly prefer the uncertainty and struggles of being free from rule over the peace and order provided by a king? Bah, good riddance, I shall withstand the desert without them.

The people packed quickly, and the caravan seemed to tremble with the anticipation of movement, like an animal yearning to run. Wooden carts were stuffed and decked with tarps. Druks were corralled out of their enclosure and guided into broad tailored yokes. Before the night fell and the chill of darkness could grab hold, the caravan set in motion.

A few people looked back. But not Bramm.

He must be a good leader, to achieve consensus like this, in the face of danger and uncertainty.

Everyone was willing to follow Bramm wherever he might lead them.

Surely, they will not venture into the desert night, the time of djinns and ghouls?

The wind began to pick up, tugging at the caravan. The king heard the story in the sound, the soliloquy of solitude. A layer of liquid formed on his eyes, not due to the pricking sand this time, but due to the sadness of impending loss.

They would. They actually would. Perhaps the time of monarchs truly is over. Perhaps there are new kings and queens, walking among the people.

Maybe this is my legacy. Maybe they are my legacy.

The king cried unabashedly.

This should not have taken a child's life. I feel the weight of the young one's death.

When the last cart rolled across the town's boundary, a tremor made people's heads turn.

The king's tower shook. From the seams between the stones, small puffs of sand emerged and coalesced into a dense curtain that obscured the tower from sight. A deep rumble.

When the sand dissipated, the tower had gone.

In withdrawal and solitude, another memory reformed.

Then king remembered one of his mentors' final visits and lessons, the last argument before the desert had swallowed the king's only remaining ancient mentor.

Many immortals had already vanished by then, including the king's family and the queen he had loved. Apprehension gripped the king, prompting him to transform his kingdom into a stronghold, impenetrable and towering in seclusion.

His mentor tried to convince him to reconsider. The old one told the king of how, even though they were immortal, they were not meant to be eternal. The greatest ruler, his mentor said, eventually obviates the necessity of his or her own being. Their subjects were the true inheritors of the earth and the salve that could tame the desert. The king had scoffed and scorned his ancient relative.

Their parting had not been not amicable and turned out to be final.

So they have some sense after all.

When the tower had vanished, and the king along with it, the people had returned. Suspicious at first, searching through all the houses and buildings.

They had forgotten that monarchs were creatures of the sand, denizens of the desert. If the king could not watch them from above, he would do so from below.

From his subterranean enclave, the king heard their footsteps, felt them live their lives. Grains of sand were the spies that kept him apprised of all that occurred in his kingdom.

He would build and protect his kingdom. He always would. But carefully now, unnoticed.

The king coerced layers of sand in intricate patterns to shepherd dew into underground canals. Soon, his people would discover a hidden source of irrigation, an oasis seemingly sprung from nothing.

When sandpard vibrations woke him from his slumber, he would lay quicksand traps.

My people will thrive. I will protect them.

They will not know. They will not supplicate. So be it. It will suffice for me.

A terrible ruler has iron hands, a good ruler velvet ones. A great ruler needs none.

"The Lonely King" originally appeared in *Metaphorosis*, on 29 November 2019

About the author

Gunnar De Winter is a biologist/philosopher who writes stories to explore ideas. Some of these stories have found their way into, for example, *Metaphorosis, Amazing Stories, Daily Science Fiction*, and various anthologies.

fictionalfieldwork.wordpress.com, @evolveon

Growing Resistance

Juliet Kemp

The late-afternoon sun hovers above the wall as I kneel on the earth, weeding tomatoes. Beyond the wall, yellow-orange light reflects off the clean sharp lines of the apartment blocks. Boxes for safe people, people who are provided for. People who matter. People who I knew, once upon a time. People who could afford the vaccine before the gates closed. The plague's gone now, but the wall's still here.

On this side, the wall's shadow stretches out as the sun sinks, spreading over the crumbling low-rise council blocks that don't get repaired any more. In between them there are patches of shanty-town on top of the spaces where the army razed houses to the ground.

My garden is on one of those bare patches, next to Mathias's and my house, which was once in the middle of a row of terraces and is now on the end. Mathias insisted we put a fence up. I planted brambles up against it so it looks less like the barrier it is. It's not like we don't share what we grow here, and I understand why Mathias did it. Still feels like a tiny echo of the wall.

Mathias is over at the community centre with the others. Talking over what they're going to do this time to try to change things. He'll tell me all about it once he gets home. I feel, again, that faint familiar guilt at not being there with him, not *helping*. But.

I straighten up from the tomato bed, and go inside to eat the half-bowl of stew I saved for myself, with some of the scavenged bread Vera brought round earlier—the stuff doesn't keep long after it's thrown out—before I do the evening chores in the drugs room.

The printer's just finished a batch of estradiol. I count the pills into their labelled wraps, clean everything out, pour in new feedstock, and start off a small batch of lithium. (Easy to print, a bugger and a half to get the precursors for.) While I'm in here, I check on the first stage of the T synthesis, sitting on the back shelf. It's coming along nicely.

One printer's not enough, but I haven't room, or time, to grow the feedstock for another, or to expand the synthesis lab.

Vera keeps telling me I need help, and specifically, that she should be the one to help. She's a good kid, Vera. Reliable. She delivers drugs for me. I first got to know her when she turned up at the door, aged fourteen, asking for puberty blockers; the health centre wouldn't give them out without parental agreement, and she didn't have a parent any more. From what she says, I brewed the antidote just in time for her, and the vaccine in time for her brother. I wasn't fast enough for their mother. Not that I knew any of them back then.

Anyway. I keep putting her off. I don't want another person to worry about. I don't want the responsibility. And she ought to have a future that doesn't involve making semi-legal drugs in a dystopian undercity; but then, oughtn't we all?

Mathias wants to fix all of this, for everyone, and goodness knows he's right. But I can't do what he does. I do what I can do, instead. I keep people alive when I can, as much as I can. That's good, right? It never feels like enough.

Mathias comes in late. I'm already in bed, almost asleep. He slides into bed next to me, wrapping an arm around me, and I wriggle back into him.

"Tell you now? Or tomorrow?" he asks, into my hair. I can feel the excitement in his body, hear it in his voice. I can't face dealing with it now.

"Tomorrow," I say, and then can't sleep anyway. I'm staring into the darkness well after Mathias is relaxed and snoring. He'll want me to join in. He'll understand when I can't. I just wish—I wish I was doing more.

It's hot again the next morning. I apply my T gel and check that Mathias has taken his insulin. Then we eat the rest of the scavenged bread for breakfast, cutting out the mouldy parts. I sip my peppermint tea and hope, like every morning, that the camellia bush thrives. I miss black tea.

"So," I say to Mathias, bracing myself. "Last night?"

"They don't see us, that's the problem," Mathias says.

It's one problem of many, but I don't interrupt.

Mathias's blue eyes light up as he leans forwards, passionate as ever. "They go in and out on the train, and stuff goes in on the train, stuff we produce, right? They rely on us, but they don't *see* us. They don't stop, they don't look, they don't have to think about it. So what if we just"—he spreads his hands—"disrupt that?"

Coming from him, it sounds obvious. Easy, even. Mathias has a gift that way.

"How?" I ask.

Mathias shrugs. "Pretty basic. Blockade the line. There's a weak point where the fence needs repair, just after where the railway comes through the wall. Vera showed me."

"Blockade how?" Visions of how this could go wrong are already blooming in my mind.

"Do you really want to know the details?" He glances down at my hands, white-knuckled around my mug.

"I want to know if I'm going to be dealing with your mangled body," I snap, louder than I'd intended. I still have nightmares about dead bodies. Not that the plague dead were mangled. Just bruised. If I'd got the lab up and running faster, they would have been fewer.

"We're barricading with stuff, wood and bricks and fencing and that, as much as we can get in there fast enough. We're not chaining ourselves to the rails," Mathias said, putting his hand on mine. "And we'll have a signal up the track. We don't want to derail the trains or hurt anyone. Just to—to make them see. It's a publicity stunt, Oak, it's not like we're going to set up a siege." His eyes go distant for a moment, calculating, before he snaps back out of it. "If people *see* our situation, if they *realise* ..."

He's more optimistic than me, but I don't want to get into the argument. I don't want to think about it anymore. I can't stop him, or any of them. I don't disagree, either. I would be there with them, maybe, if ...

"Still can't get traction for the strike?" I say instead, forcing my voice lighter.

Mathias wrinkles his nose, then sighs. "I understand why. People are scared they'll lose their scrip. This—we can do it with just the folk who are already off the books. Small but effective, you know?"

If you're in the system, if you have an ID that's authorised, you get scrip. Like money, except it's tied to your ID, and you use it to get food and medicine and that from the government outlets. Break the rules, and they dock your scrip; break them enough and they blacklist your ID and stop your scrip altogether. I could get scrip, but I don't, because I don't use my ID. Mathias got blacklisted a long time ago. Some of our people never had proper ID in the first place.

"When will it be?"

"Can't wait. They might fix that weak point. Tomorrow morning." He takes a long breath. "Oak? You wanna come out with us?

I look down at the table and shrug. "Maybe."

I don't, of course. Mathias pretends to take my 'maybe' seriously, but he doesn't look surprised when I don't come out to the final planning meeting.

It's not that I don't want to help, or that I don't think it'll achieve anything—I don't, as it happens, but that's not what's stopping me. What stops me is what happens when I think about it. I think of us breaking down the fence, and then I think of the cops showing up with batons ... and then I have to sit down and do my breathing exercises, my fingers running over the scar on my forearm, the place where the bone still aches sometimes, over and again until I make myself stop.

I'd be a burden, out there. I'd fall apart. The opposite of helpful.

I should be doing more, though. I could, if I tried harder. Should, could, should. Sometimes I wonder why Mathias puts up with me.

I water the herb garden. Marigold, feverfew, tansy, lemon balm, St John's Wort, a few more. Medical plants. The big rain barrels are running low. Maybe I should get Vera to haul me some water from the standpipe. I think about water as hard as I can, so I don't think about anything else.

Mathias kisses me next morning, before dawn, then slips out of bed. I try to go back to sleep, try to stop my brain running over everything that could already be going wrong.

We don't have net access. The neighbours do, because they're on the books, but I'd have to go out and knock on a door and ask, and yeah, that's not going to happen.

Even if I went and looked, it might not be there. Mathias might not get the publicity he wants. It might be censored. Worse, it might not need to be. It might be that no one cares. It's not like the wall's invisible. It's not like those inside it don't know already know what it's like out here, whatever Mathias might say. People choose to ignore it. They choose not to face up to the consequences of their decisions. I know those people, after all, the way Mathias doesn't. I know how they think.

A row of corn is ready for harvest and processing. I've just finished winding it through the chipper—nice hard mindless manual work—when I hear someone calling over the fence.

Vera's little brother, Joseph. Oh shit. What' s happened?

"There's a few injuries," he says, out of breath. "Mathias asked"—oh thank fuck, Mathias is okay—"if they should go to the centre or come here?"

He doesn't mean the health centre. They won't get treated there. No scrip. He means the community centre, which is bigger than our place, but my stuff's here, and I would have to pack it all up and take it over there, go be a part of things ...

I'm not a doctor, I'm a chemist, but I've learnt a bit since the wall went up. I have to be there.

"Here," I say, and tell myself, as Joseph belts off again, that it's just more convenient that way.

Mathias has broken his arm, I think, in almost exactly the same place I broke mine. Exactly the same way I broke mine, too, at a guess. Fucking cops. But he's in tearing spirits regardless. They all are. I count heads as I triage.

"This everyone?" I ask Mathias as I start splinting his arm. It's clean; it should heal okay. It might just be a bad bruise, even. Not like I have X-ray facilities here. Not like he'd get scanned if he went to the health centre.

"These are the only people injured," he says. "Everyone else got away clean."

He tells me how smoothly it all went. How they'd blocked the track, hung banners along the fence. How trains were stacking up right along the line, freight and passenger both.

"I saw loads of people taking photos," he says, all fired up, his eyes alight. "They *saw* us. They saw us."

I hope for his sake that it translates into the awareness that he wants.

"There's a photo!" Someone is waving a black-market phone around. "If it goes viral, right ...?" There's a buzz of excited conversation.

"They showed up to chase us off when we were still piling stuff up, but it was already blocked by then," Mathias tells me. "We ran for it. They didn't realise we'd made another hole 'til we were halfway through it."

Mathias and the half-dozen other bruised and battered folk sitting around the living room were the rearguard to protect the rest. No head injuries, thank goodness.

"No one arrested?" I ask, as I tie off Mathias's bandages and move onto the next patient.

"Nope," Mathias says happily.

Which is when Joseph shows up on the doorstep again, looking sick.

"Oak. Mathias. The cops have got Vera."

Vera went to look at what was happening, see how soon they'd clear it, and the cops grabbed her. She wasn't *on*

the action—Mathias wouldn't let her, because she still gets scrip, and he won't let her choose otherwise on his watch until she's eighteen—and you can't charge someone just for being nosy, even here. Not yet, anyway. They just wanted to scare her. They'll let her go.

That's not the problem. The problem is that she's sixteen, and she needs to be collected by an adult. Vera and Joseph don't have any parents. No one they know who has scrip is going to want to be associated with an arrested teenager in case they get docked or worse. No one here in this room has scrip, so that's not the problem, but anyone who goes is at risk of being arrested themselves.

But if no one shows up, Vera'll be assigned a guardian. Who knows what opinions a police-assigned guardian will have about a sixteen-year-old trans girl's hormones?

Mathias looks over at me.

I don't have scrip. And I wasn't at the action. I can't prove I was anywhere else, though, and in theory they could arrest me for the whole semi-legal medicine thing, even though that's an open enough secret that they quite clearly don't care about it. It takes the pressure off, I guess, having us manage our own damn drugs.

But I'm avoiding the point. The point is, Mathias and I both know about the ID sitting in my sock drawer.

I think about Vera, sitting there in the cop shop, not knowing what's going on. She won't have her hormones with her, either. Won't know what's going to happen next.

"She'll be okay, though, won't she?" someone says. "She's a minor, right, and she wasn't even *there* ..." His voice dies away as he sees the expressions on everyone else's faces.

He's saying what I *want* to think. I want to think that she'll be fine. That I won't have to do this.

I can't believe it, though. It's not true. Vera needs someone, and the only someone here who can do it is me. She needs me to go out there and down to the cop shop, and exert my so-called authority to get her out.

I'm breathing too fast just thinking about it. The station. The cop behind the desk. My arm hurts.

"I'll do it," Mathias says, looking at my face. He stumbles, just a little, as he stands up.

I want so badly to stay out of this. Food, medicine; those are things I can do from here, while I stay separate. This—this is *getting involved.*

"My arse you will," I say to Mathias, and pretend like my voice didn't crack.

There is no way they won't make Mathias if he shows up. He's got a recognisable voice and a broken arm; and they know him. I can't keep myself safe at Vera and Joseph and Mathias's expense, however much I want to.

It's bullshit to say this is the hardest thing I've ever done. That was the plague, by a very long way.

But I have to shut my eyes to force myself over the threshold. I used to go hiking, hours across the hills, back in the day, but the ten minute walk to the cop shop, just on our side of the wall, lurking up against it, is a whole lot further.

I want to tell Joseph, anxiously shadowing me, to sod off and leave me to it, but I let him pace me almost all the way there. I can't turn around and go back if he's with me.

I do send him away at the doorstep of the cop shop, which is when it occurs to me that I have no idea at all if I'll be able to speak when I get in there.

Well, shit. Not a lot to do but to keep moving, right?

"I'm here to collect Vera Okri," I say, when I reach the front desk. Oh look, I can talk. Well done, me.

I look at the cop's chin, not at her face, then I look down at the scratched grey plastic of the desk. I focus on my breathing. I ignore anything else, any other images, coming into my mind. They're just pictures. I can let them go. I don't let myself hold my arm.

"Were you at the disturbance this morning, then?" An attempt at a chatty tone, just-good-friends-here. Yeah, as if.

"I was not. I was at home. I've come to collect Vera." I'm going for bored, myself. I have no idea if that's coming across.

"I'm going to need to see some ID, sir."

I hate this, I hate this. I hand it over.

I'm still not looking at the cop's face, but I see the shift in her body, and I hear the change in her tone.

"Well. Of course, this is in order, uh, madam ..."

"I prefer sir," I say through clenched teeth. That's not even the thing I hate most about my ID, although I do wish I'd got it changed before everything else happened.

"Sir," she says. If I had ID from this side of the wall, she'd still be saying madam, I guarantee you.

What my ID says—what I hate most about it—is that I could walk right through that gate right now if I chose to. I don't, and I won't, because it's all fucking bullshit. The only reason I'm allowed inside is because my family bought me the vaccine. I let them do it because I hadn't realised then what it was going to mean.

The vaccine doesn't even matter anymore. We finally managed to produce it on this side—and pints of my blood went into the effort, so I suppose there was some value to the damn thing in the end—but that's not what the wall's about any more. It's about who had enough to buy themselves safety then, and who chooses to keep things this way now. The haves and the have-nots.

And my ID says I'm a have. I wanted to cut the damn thing up, but Mathias convinced me not to. He said it might come in handy sometime. And hey, look. He was right.

I still hate it. I hate that if I didn't have it, this whole thing would be going down differently.

But it means I can help Vera. There is that.

"Are you taking responsibility for the minor, then?" the cop asks.

I risk looking up. Her expression now is very different from the one I associate with cops. She's not about to hit me with anything. Not me, not right now.

Still could have been her that broke Mathias' arm.

I realise I haven't said anything. "I'm collecting Vera," I say cautiously. I don't understand what she's asking.

"I understand that her parents are dead," the cop says. "I need to allocate her to a proper guardian. She should have one already." But there's no real censure in her voice; we both know that the plague messed things up, this side of the wall. At least Vera's ID is correct; she transitioned longer ago than I did, and her mum sorted it all out back then, before everything.

Anyway. Vera didn't want a guardian, so she's managed without one. She won't want one now, either, but it looks like that's the price of getting her out of here.

"Fine," I say.

I must sound stroppy, because the cop gets apologetic. "I won't be able to, uh," she waves her hand at my ID, still lying on the counter. She means Vera won't get my privileges. "But there won't be any repercussions for her, if you're taking responsibility." She means she'll still get scrip.

We go through a whole tedious stack of paperwork. I still feel sick and my pulse is sky-high, but I'm coping.

Then Vera gets brought out through the reinforced door at the side, and we are, finally, free to go.

Vera's limping a little, but she shakes her head at me when I frown down at her leg, so we keep going, out the door. Not long now 'til I'll be home again.

"Sir!"

My heart jumps straight into my throat as I turn around.

"You forgot your ID, sir." The cop hands it back to me.

I want to hand it straight back to her. I bare my teeth in something approximating a polite smile, and put it in my pocket.

"Is this going to ..." Vera sounds subdued. "Are you in trouble?"

I pull a face, looking down at the broken pavement. "No. I got—never mind. I got immunity, kind of."

I can feel Vera squinting at me, but I'm not explaining this to her.

"You'll still get scrip, too," I add, then remember. "But, uh, she had to register you to me." I wince. "Like some kind of guardian shit, I dunno. Sorry. I guess it doesn't matter much. I'm not about to start guardian-ing you, don't worry."

Vera shrugs. "I'm out, and I've still got scrip. I'm good." She swallows. "Thanks."

I shrug. "Eh. Wasn't anything so much."

And I realise, as I say it, that I'm right. It's just paperwork. It's *wrong*, and that's important, but ... it's just bureaucracy. Not like the food, or the medicine. That's us, coming together. Me supporting people in the way that I can. From each according to their ability, and all that. The ID gives me the ability to bail Vera out when no one else could, and it matters that I did that; but everything else matters more. This is my community; and I do what I can. Maybe that is enough, after all. Maybe I can let myself be part of it.

"Heyyyy though, Oak," Vera says, drawing my attention. "If you're my guardian now, will you teach me to work the printer?"

She never gives up, this kid. I roll my eyes, and feel my pulse starting to slow. "Maybe."

Vera hears the yes behind the maybe, and grins at me.

"I've got your next month's worth of E and spiro, back at the house," I say, and she grins a bit wider. Her relief is infectious; I can feel my own shoulders going down.

Maybe. Maybe what I do does matter.

Maybe can be yes.

I step through my front door with vast relief. Mathias is in the hallway, and puts his uninjured arm around me.

"You were right to make me keep it," I say into his ear.

He kisses me.

There are more people here now; the uninjured ones have arrived, I guess. Joseph is telling Vera off, which is amusing. Someone is showing round something on a rehabbed tablet.

"We did it," Mathias tells me, gleeful. "So much publicity. People asking questions all over the net. A City politician, even. Half the shop shelves were empty this morning, too, and that's hooked into the demo photos, so that's even more coverage. That's the thing with just-in-time delivery, it's so damn easy to disrupt."

I hate what it takes for people to *see*. But if it does, if it helps …

"Good work," I say. I sigh, looking around. "I'll make stew, I guess. You've all been up since the middle of the night."

"You'll sit the hell down and *I'll* make stew," Vera says, appearing from behind Mathias; then, reacting to my look, "What? I can cook."

"Let her," Mathias advises me, and steers me to a seat.

I look around, at our living room full of people. People I know. People whose drugs I make. People whose food I grow, some of it. People who are dedicated to fixing this shitty system. Maybe I'm not doing what they are, but I'm doing something. I helped Vera. I help a lot of people. Sometimes I can't. But sometimes I can. I can be part of this.

I am, already.

I hear the printer stop in the next room. I nod at Mathias, and go through to sort this batch and get the next one running.

We're all doing something. This is my thing. These are my people. We're all in this together, trying to change it; and this is enough. I am enough.

"Growing Resistance" originally appeared in *Translunar Travelers Lounge*, on 16 August 2019

About the author

Juliet Kemp is a queer, non-binary writer who lives in London with their partners, child, and dog. Their first two fantasy books, *The Deep And Shining Dark* and *Shadow And Storm* are both available from Elsewhen Press, and their short fiction has appeared in various places. In their free time, they go bouldering, tend their towering to-be-read pile, and get over-enthusiastic about fountain pens. They can be found at http://julietkemp.com, or as @julietk on Twitter.

Rooks on Sundays

Jack Neel Waddell

"You never liked to play chess with me," she says.

The board lies on a tray across her bed. Pillows prop her up slightly, just enough to see the pieces.

She reaches out a wrinkled hand, skin both pale and blotched brown, like the flesh of an apple left out too long. She grabs a rook that she carved, perhaps twenty-five years ago, from purpleheart wood. Today she remembers how it moves.

"I know how much you love it, Mom," I say, the word still feeling awkward in my mouth. It took me weeks to even say it.

We play until the end of visiting hours. She frowns as a nurse comes in. She weakly tries to push him away as he hooks her oxygen mask back over her face, clasping the straps behind her head within the milkweed-seed wisps of her hair.

I walk out of her room and toward the door of St. Agatha's hospice.

"You have to sign out, ma'am," calls the registration nurse after me.

The log book is open, with the heading, "Patient: Ella Reilly."

I sign Katherine Reilly, the only name on the list going back every Sunday for pages.

I've hidden the case in a park a few blocks away. A few cherries are blooming, but a chilling drizzle drives away any strolling couples.

I press the button on the front of the case to return.

I tuck the case back under the bench in my garage shop. Then I get inside my Corolla and drive.

There's one other place I go on Sundays.

It isn't raining here, now. The sun shines with vernal tenderness through the willows onto a pair of monument stones, dated only months apart. I place butter-yellow mums on my dearest James's grave, the one on the right. Kay, our daughter, buried in the other, never cared for flowers.

She injured her back when a Land Rover drove her into a ditch on her way to the coffee shop. She was taking an extra shift to pay us rent, which I imposed when she refused to sign up for classes at the community college.

The doctor gave her pills, which ran out. She found more, then she took too many.

James always blamed me for the gulf between us and our daughter. He left me after Kay's funeral, but his heart gave out before the divorce was final, whether from grief or stress or coincidence.

I wish I could take my case back to one or any moment during that time, to pull them back to me. Or, if not that, just to have them again as I push them from me — an arm's length away is closer than six feet deep. But the past is Hermetically sealed, even to my machine.

I've already purchased the bare plot to the right of James, but I won't need it for twenty-eight years. Now I'm saving up for the Catholic rest home in town, the best in the county, since I will have no one to tend to me but myself, and only on Sundays.

I drive back to my shop. Small blocks of exotic wood lie scattered on the workbench. I reach for a piece of purpleheart I rounded on the lathe, then hesitate. Instead, I select ebony. I pick up a gouge and carve.

Slivers of the past fall away with each splinter. Soon I think of nothing but the piece hidden in the grain and, after a while, I finish the crenellated parapet of a rook.

"What's this?" she asks as I hand her the box. It's wide, long, and thin, like a box of chocolates.

"A gift, Mom," I say. "Open it."

She pulls the ribbon and lifts the top. Laid out in four rows is the chess set I've made over the past month, of ebony and olivewood. She picks up the kings of each color.

"They're beautiful, Kay," she says.

She smiles, eyes beaming, and it warms my heart.

"You made these?" she asks.

I nod, with a strangely proud smile spreading across my face. But her eyebrows draw together in suspicion. She turns her eyes up and left, as if she's trying to call something elusive to mind.

"Mom?"

She looks at me, and I see something change in her.

She puts the pieces back in the box and places it aside, then leans out and places a pale hand on my own. She looks into my eyes, and I into hers. I see the peanut-brown of her irises, not the forest-floor hue of Kay's, and I know she sees the same because within her eyes shines a spark of recognition. A spark that fades into sorrow.

"You're so good to visit me," she says, voice breaking. "All we've got is each other."

"Rooks on Sundays" originally appeared in *Metaphorosis*, on 1 November 2019

About the author

Jack Neel Waddell is a Southern writer, physicist, and educator. He lives with his wife, baby, and furred companions in Arkansas, where he enriches young minds (but only to reactor-grade levels, he swears). His fiction has previously appeared in *Strange Economics* anthology, *The Colored Lens*, and the *SQ Mag Best of the Year* anthology, among others. You can find him occasionally at gildthetruth.wordpress.com.

gildthetruth.wordpress.com, @OrnaVerum

The Trader

Damien Krsteski

1.

Machine guns fire and mortars blossom on the brickwork house up ahead. Marko ducks underneath a bridge from which combatants shoot and lob grenades; he hurries down the alley.

The frail scent of garlic and parsley and beetroot from his grocery bag is smothered by the tinge of artillery smoke wafting in from the river quay; gun patter follows the stench, and he decides to avoid the riverside and take the roundabout way home through an abandoned residential neighborhood. Posters of warring factions, half of which he doesn't even recognize, fleck the walls there. Always new ones: fresh recruits, splinter groups, or newly-formed battalions cobbled together from bits of those recently dismantled, there's always somebody eager to pry a weapon from cold hands and pick up the fight. Beyond their names, he knows nothing about these factions, wants to know nothing about them, *must know nothing* if he is to succeed.

The dull booms of far-off explosions echo in the muddy yard enclosed by flaking high-rises, and Marko cuts through. A deflated football caked with mud lies on the gravel. Marko stops, prods the football with a toe, picks it up and tucks it away in his bag, thinking he may be able to sew it back together, breathe life into it and trade it for fresh produce at next week's market.

With the city's population having dwindled shortly after the outbreak of the war due to violent death or migration (for the luckier few), most buildings remain empty, bereft of life and light. And so it is with Marko's own high-rise, which he has to himself, all thirty-five stories of it, though he mainly occupies one tiny bit half-way up, a single bedroom condo with a view to the river. And there's no bolt or padlock on his door, unlike the doors of the few Remainers he's seen, only the same old knob lock he's had since he moved in as a student, opened with the same key.

He walks in, the moldy smell of the apartment a relief, a comfort, because he's made it home safely once more, but then he gasps, dropping the bag of groceries.

In his living room, a tall figure straightens up, one hand outstretched with a gun trained on Marko.

"Where are they?" the man says, the voice distorted and chopped up into even syllables, kept out of reach for most speech recognition software. His face hides behind a gas mask, which lengthens it, lending him a fox-like appearance.

"Where's what?"

"Don't play dumb. You know who I am. What I'm capable of."

"I do," Marko says, although in truth he doesn't; the man could belong to any faction.

"I'm not going to ask you a second time."

Marko slumps his shoulders. He quickly assesses the situation and concludes that his best chance of surviving this encounter will be to take the man to his stash, so he turns around and motions for the man with the gun to follow.

"No funny business," the man says.

They go out into the hallway and take the stairs up for seven floors. On the twenty-ninth floor, he takes his captor to the door of apartment 34D, in whose lock Marko slides a metal bolt, rattles it around, and the door pops open. He gestures for the man to go in. "Take whatever it is that you require," Marko says and leans against the corridor wall.

He hears the man whistle in amazement, then curse, then kick the boxes filled with found or traded goods, once, twice, stronger this time, as if to make them spill their contents on the ground. Cardboard torn open; the uncouth captor clawing and digging through Marko's possessions, his hard-earned currency. Once the man's done going over the wares, he steps out, gun to Marko's temple. "Who do you work for?"

"Myself."

"Don't be funny," the man says, words diced up as if spoken through a spinning fan, "or I'll paint this here wall a funny brain color. Who do you work for?"

"I told you: nobody."

"You hoard all that shit for *nobody*? You traded ten shells and promised ten more by the end of the week. But you have two boxes of the stuff already. What's your game, huh?"

The grenade shell deal, Marko realizes, meaning this must be a representative of the Red Moth Squad. Or is that the Raptor Rapture Boys, and the Red Moths are the ones who placed an order for candle wax and sulfur ampules?

The man presses harder with the gun, so Marko says, "There's no game, I give you what I can afford." The rest, he finishes the sentence in his head, goes to other clients demanding the product, clients who are accorded their ration based on his careful calculations.

"You shit," the man hisses, "who else do you do work with?"

"Work with?"

"Trade. Make deals." The man taps his foot; tremors pass through his body, but his gun-hand remains steady.

Marko deliberates, taking the man's composure into account, his grip on the gun, his raspy, pitch-corrected breathing, then he decides it's in his own best interest to tell the truth. "Everybody," he says. "I trade with all of you."

The man pauses. Marko can't see his eyes, can't see his face, but the man's body shifts ever so slightly, and the pressure of the gun on Marko's temple loosens. "Liar," the man says.

"No," Marko says, "that I'm not. What I am is a survivor. Which is solely because of my goods and my work."

The Red Moth or Raptor Boy quickly glances at the boxes as if to make sure these goods and this work are still real, still there, then he says, "Okay, okay, old man, you work for everybody, so get ready to face the consequence of feeding my enemies." And he pulls his head back, bracing for the gunshot.

Marko cringes, shuts his eyes, and says, "But where will that put you, Red Moth?" He takes a gamble with the gang name, which ends up paying off: the man doesn't correct him but cocks his head slightly. "Cutting off the supply line of more than two-thirds of the city's combatants; how smart would that be, I wonder? You think everyone hates everyone now, but once word gets around that a Moth had disrupted the chain of supply— and word will inevitably get around, believe you me, when those death-switch trade logs of mine are released —your faction will lose all its allies, and the *bellum omnium contra omnes* will effectively end, turning into a manhunt. And you will be found. And you will be murdered. Or worse." And suddenly, as if to drive Marko's point home, three strong booms thunder in from outside, from somewhere beyond the river, and the man winces.

"Bullshit," he says, releasing the safety of the gun. But he stands there, and then again he says to himself, "Shit," and he lowers the gun somewhat. "Fuck." The chopped up words, no longer threatening, begin to sound comical.

"I am sorry," Marko says, meaning it.

The Moth takes one more glance at the boxes inside the storeroom, longingly, most likely, if only one could see beneath that vinyl mask, then he disappears behind the staircase door, footfalls stomping as he takes several steps at a time, and Marko slumps on the floor and cups his face. He lets out a long, slow, quivering breath.

He will have to abandon this place within twenty-four hours, and move, and get lost, lugging what goods he can carry to another hideout from where he can proceed with his work.

He realizes he's shaking. He doesn't have much time. He has to go pack.

But first he gets up and drags himself back into his apartment, and he picks up the beets that have rolled off under his couch, and he puts them in a pot and stirs the cold water, adding a sprig of parsley and a sprinkle of powdered garlic, and he makes a thick vegetable gazpacho for dinner.

2.

He packs up whatever it is that he can carry and leaves, his apartment left behind with the door ajar like all the others nestled in this high-rise, all the others in this city, abandoned shelters claimed by decay where mold replaces what once may have been warmth. Through the damp tunnels of the subway he makes his way, ankle-deep in mud and feces, pulling by rope an old ironing board on which he's strapped his indispensable supplies and a select few trade goods. Popping out to breathe the even fouler air of the city, scouting out the terrain, then diving back down into the subway tunnels where his feet follow the railway line when there—in chunks that haven't been torn out and sold for scrap—beneath the thick layer of excrement. No longer the invulnerable everyman hidden behind the facade of a poor Remainer but a ripe target for raiders, it takes him three days to make it safely across town to the hideout he had once built for an occasion very much like this one.

Near the city's old football stadium, whose concrete rim is dented and chipped away like a dead man's jawline, lies his bunker, which he can now see, its manhole-like aperture hidden behind a thicket of branches. It is from here that he will continue to fight against this war, because he must, otherwise this madness will go on forever and ever and the bodies will stack up like high-rises, emptying and molding and rotting.

Marko clears the branches and gingerly pops the cover open, and first he lowers his wares-studded ironing board down into the safe-house, then he himself climbs down the ladder, and when his feet touch the ground he looks around and finds the place odd, changed, the books on his shelves slightly tilted to one side, a jar of marmalade left open on the table by the mattress, the papers on his escritoire shuffled about. He takes a few tentative steps, peeks behind corners, but finds nobody, finds the place as deserted as the day he finished construction. Perhaps some raiders had discovered it a while ago and had poked around; but then why would they leave the storeroom with the supplies virtually intact?

The hatch above opens again, and a figure slides down the side of the ladder, dropping like a coat off a hanger. "Who are you?" The shaft of light falls on a knife; a glint, a flicker, as the hand jabs the air with the weapon.

Marko flinches, then says, "I'm—I'm the one who built—this place."

"Well, now it's mine." A pair of almond eyes, milky white, staring at him. "Go away."

"I can't," he stutters, "I can't leave."

"Go or I will make you go." The voice is a woman's voice, Marko realizes—a girl's voice.

"I already left one place. I can't leave another. Not this soon."

The girl stands there, crouching, knife-hand outstretched, and somehow Marko knows she won't do him harm; not because she seems incapable of killing, but because she seems incapable of killing an unarmed man. And sure enough, a few intense moments later, she growls as if scolding herself and tucks the knife away in her belt. "What's your name?"

"Marko."

"Marko," she repeats.

"Yes. And yours?"

"What faction, Marko?"

"No faction. I live alone and survive alone."

"Bullshit," she says. "Nobody survives alone."

"You seem to have."

Which makes her reach for her knife again. She doesn't unsheathe it, just pats the blade. "Don't presume anything, Marko."

"I've lived in this city my whole life, and when the troubles started to unfold, I elected to remain and do what I do best."

"Which is?"

"Making do."

For the first time the girl moves in a non-threatening way, a small stroll to the mattress and back, circling him, almost as if to mark territory. She's shorter than him. And very young. "And what does that entail?"

"Collecting. Rationing. Trading," he says, then, pointing to the shelf with the row of books askew, he adds, "You've been reading my books."

She quickly glances at the books then back at him, and in the dark, dark of the bunker, with only an inkling of light from the shaft by the ladder, he sees her blush. "What sort of trading?"

"Which was your favorite? Did you enjoy *Reflections of a City in the Mirror*? Or was the poetry of Babic more to your liking? Or Mr. Domovin's parables?"

"If you don't answer I will gut you."

"I traded with all factions. I found or bought goods and traded them for other goods, building up a stash. I calculated who needed what and allowed for the factions, essentially, to trade amongst themselves through me."

"So," she says, "you had contact with all of them?"

"Most factions, yes."

She comes closer to study his face, then pulls back again. "Why are you here now?"

"Because they found my living quarters. My stash. Which was dangerous. The Trader never revealed his identity and location, but worked with drone drop and pickup spots only." The girl stares at him blankly, so he adds, "And by the Trader I mean myself."

"I got that," she says.

"May I ask why *you* are here?"

"You may not." She circles him once, twice, as if deliberating what to do with him. "But here I will have to stay for a day or five at least," she says, "so question is, what to do with you?" She goes around him two more times, clockwise, then contrariwise, arms by her sides.

"I won't be an issue."

"You already are."

"I mean to say, I won't bother you more than with my presence."

"Why shouldn't I just chuck you out with that ironing board of yours? Leave you to sleep on some bench."

"Because," he says, "you won't even know I'm here. All I need is my desk and my notebooks to begin with. And because it's cold and dangerous out there, and I have done you nothing to deserve that."

She considers his words for a moment, then sits down on the chair by the escritoire and considers them some more. She sighs. Rubs her eyes. "Fine," she says. "Fine."

"Thank you."

"But one wrong move," she says and pats her knife again.

Marko nods and tells her that he is exhausted after days of travel and his legs can't carry him anymore, and she tells him she is, too, and they better sleep, but she informs him that she will sleep with one eye open and that she won't be sharing the mattress with him and that the floor is all his. To prove her point, she throws him a bundle of dirty rags, which, when he lies on the ground, he wads up and places under his head.

"Sleep tight," he says.

She doesn't reply, but a moment later she says, "*Reflections*." She clears her throat. "That was my favorite." And she turns to the side, patting her dusty pillow, and starts snoring within minutes.

When he wakes up, the girl's gone.

His cracked wristwatch, which he wears on his left ankle, tucked away from prying hands, tells him it's minutes to six. He rubs his eyes, stretches, and sets to work, starting with unwrapping the layers of duct tape off his mummified luggage strapped to the ironing board, then airing out everything until the stench of the subway tunnels is reduced to a whiff, and finally he sits at his escritoire and performs a general review of his folders of documents under the dim light of an old, flickering, battery-run desk lamp. He has brought carbon-copies of his work here, too, but not everything— a lot of the mathematics had been done on that apartment's walls and floors, mimicking Teacher in her way of surrounding herself with the work, being constantly reminded; luckily he has with him the notebook containing his work's first principles from which he can build the whole system back up again. He scrawls in the margins, jotting down notes and calculations to factor in his newly-diminished position, until he loses all track of time: he will need to start with the basics—tin, copper, water, gunpowder—and work his way up to the rarer supplies, then the stronger explosives and ammunition, then the prestigious, luxurious items will follow, and then he will be able to play the factions against themselves as he sees fit, and tip the scales of the war, and force all factions to retreat, to defend, to surrender.

The hatch creaks open, and by the time Marko lifts his eyes from his equations the girl's feet are on the floor. She pulls on the cord, shutting the hatch. White light turns yellow.

"Brought something," she says, and throws a box of old crackers on the mattress.

"Where did you find those?"

"Out there."

At last he says, "Thanks."

She nods toward the storeroom with the jars and cans of preserved food. "I didn't mean to steal," she says. "The first night, when I was starving, I borrowed some biscuits and slathered them with marmalade. So there. I pay you back." She lies on the mattress, hands behind her head. "I'm no thief."

"Never thought you were," he says. "Thank you."

"Anja," she says.

"Thank you, Anja."

Within three days, he sets up a new trading network and starts amassing supplies.

Marko reaches out to former points of contact and sends them word of his situation through the only remnant of the erstwhile civilization: those featureless automated drones buzzing among the ruins of the city, picking up and dropping off parcels to encrypted addresses known only to them and the sender, slaloming through the city airspace to shake off any would-be tracers, allowed, by an unvoiced agreement between all factions, to exist and be useful for all. His initial trading contacts respond within hours with lists of the current status of demand/supply on the market in their side of town, and he quickly scribbles notes with what he has to offer, and stuffs them in the claws of the drones before their stuttering rotors whisk them away.

He scours the area around the bunker for scrap, for useful bits of material, but finds slim pickings; this is the eastern half of the city, the formerly busy and chic neighborhoods clustered around the old park with the stadium, which means it was the first to be stripped of anything of value.

The girl he sees only at night when she returns, exhausted and quiet, knife in her teeth, from wherever it is that she roams; he doesn't dare ask.

One night, following a day of extensive and mind-numbing work, which proves more daunting now that he has to consider how his backlog of orders from his stash have failed to be disseminated among the rival factions, he nods off over his book, dreaming in snapshots of Teacher and the life before all this, snapshots flashing like white phosphorus across the sky, snapshots cut short by the bang of the hatch. He shakes his head and finds drool over his shirt, his book.

Anja climbs down the ladder one rung at a time, cursing to herself. She drags herself to the mattress, and only when she gasps and grimaces, hand pressing her abdomen, does Marko realize that she's hurt.

"What happened?"

"None—of your business."

"You're hurt. Let me have a look." He takes a step toward the mattress, but she raises a hand, wincing. He says, "This is idiotic, you're hurting." He ignores her gesture and takes whatever it is that resembles first-aid supplies from his storeroom and kneels down by the mattress.

Sweat dapples Anja's pale yellow face. He lifts up her shirt to the belly-button and sees a cut the length of his thumb, blood bubbling out of it, but one that's not a deep gash, fortunately. He soaks up the blood with a dry rag, then dabs at the wound with another rag doused in the only disinfectant he could find, pure pre-war vodka, and finally duct-tapes a thin strip of gauze over the cut.

He makes her drink water and eat canned peach slices, and when he asks her what had happened, she groans, says she doesn't want to talk about it, and the blood loss and exhaustion take their toll and she falls asleep. Marko watches over her while she sleeps, listening to her shallow breaths, reading a book in one hand. When some hours later she comes to, she says she's ready to go back out.

"There's no way you're going out there in this shape."

"I told you," she says, "it's none of your business what I do, how I do it, and when I decide to do it. Which in this case, is right this very moment." But she props herself up and then drops her head back down on the pillow, grimacing in pain.

"Like I said, there is no way."

Anja fixes him a dirty look, then she sighs, and says, nodding toward the books, "Fine, then give me one of those."

"Why do you trade," she says, looking up from her book, "when you don't keep anything for yourself, when you're always poor?" She makes a sweeping, all-encompassing gesture with one hand to prove her point.

"Because I don't want anything for myself."

"What do you want, then?"

"I want to this to end."

She gives him a puzzled look. "Which faction?"

"None of them to win, all of them to lose." He scratches his cheek. "I am balancing things out, smoothing the wrinkles, slowly making all factions equal in strength, and then I bleed them weaker, simultaneously, none more so than any other, and then I bleed them dead."

"Even the Goldmouths?"

"Even the Goldmouths."

"But—but they are not *bad*. Not like others."

"I don't know what the Goldmouths are fighting for."

"How the hell can you not?"

"Because I don't know what any of them are fighting for, and I don't want to know, because only then I can remain impartial and do my work well. All I know is I can stop them, and we will breathe clean air in this city again."

It takes Anja little to no time to get back on her feet, to be up and about and trawling the city during the day, but now their evenings have changed, because they talk more, and they read together, sometimes even out loud to each other. One night Anja offers him the mattress, saying they should maybe switch and she should sleep on the floor a while, but he steadfastly refuses, lying that he's now so used to the planks and rags that he wouldn't even manage to get a wink of sleep on anything softer.

3.

Anja returns from one of her city escapades angry, cursing. When she calms down somewhat, she tells him, "You have to tell me how to get in. In the nest of Blackstars."

"Are you crazy?"

"You have to tell me. You have traded with them."

"Is that where you've been going all this time?"

"I told you," she says, and her eyes turn ruby red, "where I go is none of your goddamn business."

She hasn't spoken to him like this since their first day. She stomps her feet on the bunker planks.

"Were they the ones who hurt you? The Blackstars are dangerous."

"I know they're dangerous," she says. "I've seen them kill." Tears come to her eyes, and she blinks and they stream down her face. "And I will get to them. And get them back for that. And you will tell me how to get in."

Marko takes a step but she raises her hand. He says, "I don't know how to get in. I've only sent drones with supplies to their quarter."

"You're useless." And she crumples up a sheet of his mathematics from the escritoire and throws it at him. "A useless old man who does nothing but sit and write." And she places a foot on the ladder.

"Wait," he says, "don't go. The Blackstars will hurt you. Please, stay."

"The Blackstars," she hisses, "killed my mother, and I can't let that go. And you can't stop me, because you don't even know what they're fighting for, you don't even care. To you they're just numbers on a piece of paper, just parts of an equation, and you weren't there when she was hurting, and when she was dying, and you have no right to tell me how to handle that." And she goes up the rungs of the ladder, her knife in her teeth, and out the bunker and into the city.

On his moldy mattress he lies, thumbing through his worn notebook where equations stud the margins and weighted graphs span the pages like spiderwebs, representing the connections he's drawn among the various combatants, each with their strengths and weaknesses and supplies factored in in red ink, and he himself, somewhere in those equations, nudging one faction against another, bringing this god-awful war, in theory, closer to an end.

He gingerly closes his notebook, wrapping a blackened shoelace around it.

The girl, he knows, will have to be factored in, too, a pugnacious, ineluctable faction of one. Blackstars in long vinyl overcoats and rabbit-eared masks facing the wrath of a hurt young girl, and her, the Gang of Anja, slashing with the serrated blade, ripping into her enemies, not tip-toeing around but playing hopscotch on his weighted mathematical graphs. Stomping his theories into the ground. Because Marko finds himself no longer worrying about this war and this city and these blood-thirsty groups that are ravishing it for reasons beyond his understanding, but about one damaged person, one hurt and good and *salvageable* person, and suddenly his clarity is gone, his work tarnished.

And he finds himself needing Teacher, needing her advice, her wisdom. Somebody has to convince him to see things clearly again; to not get bogged down into human minutiae, into the pathetic fate of One, but to gawk wide-eyed at all around him and to put it all back together the way it was. So he gets up and throws his threadbare long-coat on and storms out, crossing half the city to Teacher's last known location.

The old bus station rots away with the carcasses of rusted chassis strewn about, creaking; Marko circles this humming graveyard once, approaching the building as predator does prey, then kicks a busted door open and goes in. Stench of things long-dead hits his nose and he covers half his face with the crook of his arm, and explores Teacher's last hide-out just like that, eyes squinting, elbow out. He hasn't seen her in years, and she's older than him by a decade to begin with, at the very least, and very few Remainers stay in place for long, so the futility of his gesture is not lost on him, but a claw still rips through his chest when he goes into Teacher's old room—that cabin for the announcer of bus departure and arrival times, a microphone protruding from a desk like a poised viper—and the claw rips into his heart when he finds Teacher's room empty and nondescript, with her mathematical scribbles on the teal plaster walls scratched off, ruined, the plus signs all lengthened into crosses.

He stands there, vertiginous for a brief moment, before reality seeps in and he realizes what's happened to Teacher and to her work and to his work and to this city.

And then tears come to his eyes and he sobs there boxed in in Teacher's last written lesson for him, and he remembers all those passionate sessions of her explaining the basic mathematics of her theory that the pen truly is mightier than the sword, of how one can end this war with no guns but equations if only one abstracts oneself from everything, sheds one's interest and ego and puts one's mind to the Work, and if one hopes. Which Teacher seems to have forgotten or given up on, and that makes Marko sob even harder, and before he leaves the old rotting bus station and returns to his bunker, he places one palm on the teal plaster wall and caresses the scratch-marks and kisses the scratch-marks and says, "Thank you."

4.

He takes only what he truly needs, water, a pack of biscuits, and his improvised first-aid kit consisting of a wad of bandages and half a bottle of vodka, and he leaves his bunker for the last time. In his bag, he carries *Reflections of a City in the Mirror* for her.

Nearing Blackstar territory, the city closes up, thickens, becomes hard to squeeze through alive; mines go off and barbed wire snatches those scurrying away from explosions, and Marko knows all this because he has sold them those mines, that barbed wire, so he treads carefully, sweeping the road ahead with the needled branch of a pine. The rat-tat-tat of a machine gun makes him flinch, but he walks on, scouting out the terrain for the girl who's thrown herself at these maniacs, armed with nothing but a knife.

When night falls and the sky turns the color of burning coal, he retreats into a decrepit building and huddles in a corner. Wind howls through broken windows, booms fail to die down, but his bones and muscles and ears quickly adapt, and he sleeps. Air-chopping staccatos of a delivery drone wake him up with a start; a black buzzard, against the backdrop of a gray sky, leers at him through a broken window for a wink before flying away, and Marko blinks and remembers where he is. He's wide awake; it's dawn. He quickly gathers his gear and continues his search for Anja.

His boots raise little plumes of soot as he treads on streets blanketed with ash and debris, and an eerily quiet morning creeps up on the city, on this quarter, this home of the Blackstars, and he slows, stops, takes a good look around: high-rises with gaping broken windows, the small playgrounds in between, the see-saws with their seats stolen slowly moving in the wind, up and down, up and down.

She can't be far. And they can't be far.

Then, almost as if in answer to his thought, two sets of footsteps from somewhere, an echo bouncing off the high-rises, and two men armed with machine guns emerge from below ground—dead men brought back to life—and approach him.

"Give us one good reason," one says, wiggling his bunny ears, "not to shoot you right here, right now."

Marko says, "I am not looking for trouble."

"Too late," says the other, raising his gun.

"I just want to find her."

"Find who?"

"The girl."

The two men look at each other. The first one says, "What's she to you?"

"She," Marko says, and his knees buckle and he almost drops to the ground, but instead he forces another breath of foul city air into his lungs. "She's a girl. She's just a girl, and that's all she is, and that's all she should be allowed to be, and I can't let this happen to her. She's just a little girl."

Again, a glance between themselves. "You're a senile old man. But we can let you pick who gets to shoot you."

"No," he says. "I'm not."

"Oh, aren't you?"

"Those guns. Those weapons. I gave them to you. Don't you see? I am the Trader."

"What bullshit is this?"

And he racks his brains to remember the trade logs and he rattles out the Blackstars' last purchases as proof, and the two men listen and just stare, wiggling their ears. "And if you give me the girl," he says, regaining his composure, "I will leave town and leave my stash to you, Blackstars."

The two men stand there, the butts of their rifles pressing against their shoulder blades, muzzles aimed at his chest, then one turns to the other and says something in Blackstar patois, then the other nods, and the first leaves to disappear into the ground down invisible steps. The one with the gun trained on Marko stands in silence, waiting, and when the first one reemerges, he says, "What's to say you're not lying?"

"If I'm lying, then what have you got to lose? One silly girl? But if I'm not, then you have much to gain."

The two confer again in their dialect, then one nods, and tells Marko to wait. He plunges into the depths of the earth and comes up a moment later with Anja, pale and bruised and bleeding, slung over his shoulder. He drops her to the ground in front of Marko with a thud, and places one boot on her breasts. "Now, Trader, where is that stash of yours?"

He gives them his old address and explains how to get to apartment 34D, and the two men nod, and one raises his rifle at Marko and says, Boom, and before leaving them there, the other says, "I hope our paths won't cross, Trader."

The sky, a salmon-pink backdrop painted red and black in flickers as explosives go off in the valley below. Anja's slumped on his shoulder like a sandbag, bleeding through her bandages down his chest. Marko watches the festering city struggle with itself, unmade and scattered into infinite pieces of rubble, its maw devouring its tail, and he rubs his eyes and turns away from the scorching heat and from what he's failed to save and toward a new horizon, and he grips Anja firmly and starts to walk, thinking maybe one is good enough.

"The Trader" originally appeared in *Score – an SFF symphony*, on 2 March 2019

About the author

Damien Krsteski writes science fiction and develops software. His stories have appeared in *Beneath Ceaseless Skies*, *New Myths*, *Metaphorosis*, *Mithila Review*, *The Future Fire*, and others.

monochromewish.blogspot.com, @monochromewish

The Soul Farmer's Daughters

Kyle Kirrin

Thirteen souls flit about in mason jars on the mantle above my workbench. They're bright—luminescent, even—but they're not potent enough for the Duke.

I glance at the ghostly light flickering within Vella's abdomen, then pull another stool up next to mine. "Come, sit. I've got a surprise for you."

She joins me. "But isn't—"

"He's still a little ways out. We've got time." Seventeen minutes to be exact, I think, but never say. "Close your eyes."

Vella clinks her brass eyelids shut.

"No peeking," I say, though my daughter has never peeked, not once in these six-and-a-half centuries. I pause in the interest of consistency, then reach under my workbench and flip a switch. Electricity arcs through the coils overhead, branches across the ceiling and leaps into the automaton I stashed behind a transformer some hours earlier. It sits up, stands, clomps over. "Okay. You can look."

She cocks her head. "It's...it's me?"

"Almost," I say.

"I don't understand."

I smile. Of the many moments we share time and time again, this one is my favorite, because she will never love me more than she will in this instant. "You've always wanted a little sister, right Vella?"

She jumps to her feet and her stool clatters to the floor behind her. "You mean..."

"I do. You can even pick her soul out yourself if you'd like. I doubt the Duke will miss just one."

She throws her arms around me, buries her face in my aluminum chest. "I actually get to go inside?" she says. "Oh, Father! Thank you! Thank you thank you thank you."

I squeeze her so tightly that her porcelain skin cracks beneath my fingers. My heart revs, winds down; this will be the last time she hugs me.

I boot up my viewing screens and fiddle with the dials until Vella comes into focus, click-clacking across the wasteland with an empty jar cradled to her chest as if it's already precious.

Off in the desolation behind her, the city's clock towers loom like the teeth of some giant, half-buried gear. The Duke's dirigible bobs above them, smoking, a bloated fly that seems to swell with each breath I take.

Vella opens the outer hatch to the Soularium and gags at the stench that seeps out—as she always does—then slips inside.

I flip a toggle, and the stream jumps to the glass dome, where 144 humans dangle from ceiling-mounted chains in twelve orderly rows.

Solar panels jut wing-like from each of their backs, and hydration tubes snake down their throats. Simulators cover their eyes and ears and noses and mouths.

I tap the intercom. "Can you hear me?"
Vella's voice crackles back: "Father, what is this?"
"This is how souls are made, Vella."
"But they're—"

"Suffering? Of course they are. You can't forge a soul without pain. We've talked about this."

"But this is different, seeing them. This is so much worse than I thought it'd be."

"I know, sweetheart. I know. But best be quick. The Duke's almost here."

She stares down at her feet. "How do I know which soul to pick?"

"There's always some guesswork involved," I say, "but as far as people are concerned, the eyes are your best shot. Remember: the sharper the pain, the greater the sacrifice, the grander the soul."

"So..."

"You'll have to remove their visors to check."

"Ah."

"Think of your sister. We'll be a real family, Vella. That's what you want, right?"

She nods and sets the jar on the floor with trembling hands. "Alright. Okay." She steps up to a human and peels the simulator off his face. His bloodshot eyes find hers. He opens his mouth, but Vella slams the simulator back on before he has a chance to speak. "I can't do this. This is, this is—"

"You can. Try another one. Just one more."

Vella takes a shuddering breath and plucks another visor off a nearby human. This woman doesn't beg, doesn't scream. She doesn't even twitch. She just stares straight ahead, glassy-eyed, hollowed out.

As if on cue, Vella's hands curl into fists. She looks up into the camera, at me, with hardening eyes. "What do they see?"

"Whatever it is that they need to see."

"That's not enough," she says. "That's not even close to enough." She places the simulator to her own face.

This time, I remember to cut the audio a split-second before Vella screams. She drops to her knees, heaving, oil gushing out of her throat. I reconnect the audio.

The human looks on, unblinking, a scarecrow wrapped in sallow flesh.

Vella wipes the back of her hand across her oil-slicked lips. "Father, this isn't okay."

"No, but it's necessary. Please, Vella, take the soul —he's here."

Vella glances up through the glass ceiling, where the underbelly of the Duke's hulking dirigible is blotting out half the sky. "Does it ever stop?" she says.

"Does what stop?"

"After he harvests them. Does it stop? The pain."

"No," I say, the lie slipping smoothly off my tongue. "It never stops. But we need souls, Vella. Or there'd be no sisters, no children, nothing. We'd all be statues, shells."

Her eyes flick to the pyrolysis lever that's oh-so-conveniently mounted on the wall beside her.

I zoom in and watch her face. As always, I'm looking for aberrations, for some blessed malfunction in her code to base my hopes on. For a sign, however insignificant, that things aren't about to play out the way they always do. Because if Vella were defective, I might be able to justify keeping her. But once again, she's perfect.

"I know what you're thinking," I say, "but this is ten years' worth of work. Enough souls to populate a city. We're worth it, aren't we?"

"No," she says, and there is steel in her voice. "We aren't. Nothing should have to suffer like this." She wraps her delicate fingers around the lever.

"Please don't leave me," I say. Then, quieter: "not again."

Of the many moments we share, this is the one I despise most: the moment where—for the sixty-seventh time—Vella recognizes me for one infinitesimal part of the monster I really am.

"I still love you," she says, but she's always been a terrible liar. She squeezes her eyes shut and flips the switch.

Fire fills the dome. And just like that, it's over. What's left of the humans dusts the floor; their now-empty shackles swing freely from the ceiling; their souls scatter like cinders, reddening the glass where they flutter up against it.

But Vella still stands, glowing white-hot, her molten skin trickling down her frame and pooling around her feet.

And burning brighter than all of that—brighter than the flames, than the Duke's halogens, than even the stars themselves—is Vella's soul, a ball of liquid light that's illuminating her from the inside out.

"Father?" she says. "Why am I fireproof?"

"I'm sorry," she says again, as the Duke's ship touches down.

"You did the right thing," I say. "You always do the right thing."

"I don't understand."

"Every single time. I so wish you'd do the wrong thing, just once. Maybe then we'd have the sort of life we've always dreamed of. A real one."

"What do you mean, real?"

The cabin opens up and a ramp drops into the dirt. The Duke clatters towards us, just a head and torso mounted on eight spidery legs. Two of his automatons follow in his skittering wake.

"Is the girl ready for harvest?" the automatons say as one.

"She is," I say.

Vella presses a hand to her exposed abdomen. "You mean—it's my soul he's after? But—"

The automatons stomp towards her in lockstep.

"But I said I was sorry," Vella says. "Father, please! You still love me, don't you?"

"You served your purpose well," I say.

The automatons grab her by her arms and haul her away. I force myself to meet Vella's eyes. To watch her reevaluate the lie of a life I gave her. To watch her learn to hate me. The look on her face eviscerates what's left of my heart, just like it's supposed to.

A door seals shut behind her, and I know I'll never see that iteration of her again. The automatons will dispose of her body along with her soul; it, too, is much too weak for the Duke.

"Thank you, brother," the Duke says.

"I'm not doing this for you," I say, yet again, because it reminds me of what's at stake.

"I know," he says. "But I'm still sorry, for what it's worth."

I shrug and wipe my eyes, out of habit rather than necessity. I have no tears left to shed.

"I can't imagine reliving these same ten years," my brother says, "knowing this day will come." He presses a leg to my shoulder. "You're a hero back home, truly. Father would be proud."

I shake him off.

"Do you need a moment?" he says.

"I'm fine."

He nods. "Business then. I assume we're still on schedule?"

"We are." I pry my chest plate open and the Duke flinches away from the searing light that flares from me. My incandescence makes the dusky glow of his own failing soul seem utterly insubstantial; he has only eight-hundred years left at most.

"We must be getting close," he says, shielding his eyes with a thin pair of legs. "How many more loops before the donor soul's complete?"

"Twenty-two," I say, and the number leaves me leaden.

Twenty-two more Vellas; twenty-two more final hugs; twenty-two more I still love yous, all to delay my brother's death.

No—to prolong his rule. Because merciless as he might be, the Duke's hand is steady, and these last two millennia have been the most peaceful our clockwork city has ever known.

And because even after so many centuries, I can still picture Vella—the real, original Vella—crumpled on the sidewalk, her once-bright soul guttering around the fragments of her shattered chest. Vella, whose only crime was proximity to a riot she had no hand in.

I suck a breath through my aching throat. "How are things back home?"

"Tenuous," he says, "but manageable. Word's just gotten out that I won't be expiring as everyone expected —so the more ambitious factions are threatening revolution—but I've got it under control." He folds his legs underneath him and lowers himself to my level. "You'll come back with me once we're done here, won't you?"

"I should get the next loop going," I say.

He sighs, shakes his head. "As you wish. But tell me, brother: how do you do it?"

"Because when I do bring Vella back for good, I want there to be a world left for her to return to. Her future is worth the price."

"That's not what I meant. I founded nine new farms at the turn of this century, but none of them have yet to produce a soul that's lasted beyond two decades."

"Sounds like the farmers aren't taking to their offspring."

"Likely so. But how do you do it? How do you make yourself love them?"

"I've never had to try."

There is no laughter to be heard in my workshop now, no exaggerated sighs, no tapping of restless feet. Just a silence that feels not only smothering, but deserved.

I busy myself with the incinerator, starting with the belongings Vella left behind. Her decorative panels, her dolls, her colored irises. The clockwork dog I've always promised to bring to life but never have.

I'm about to burn her notebook when its weight gives me pause; it's heavier than ever before. I crack it open and flip through one familiar drawing after the next until I find the culprit: a piece of loose-leaf jammed between two pages. A new picture. The first ever aberration in the pattern since the Duke and I first set to harvesting my heartbreak almost seven-hundred years ago.

In her drawing, Vella and I are standing just outside the Soularium, and the Duke's dirigible floats a few feet off the ground. She and I are holding hands, and it is impossible to say whether the ship is landing or leaving.

The aberration is almost certainly nothing. It could just be a residual memory, a product of generational transference, some small corruption in the coding of her latest departed soul.

Regardless, I smooth the picture out and slip it into the drawer of my workbench. I've already decided that the dirigible she drew is taking off.

I snatch a copy of Vella's soul off the mantle and slot it into the automaton's abdomen. I dash back to my workbench and begin a diagnostic of her vital parameters, I test the articulation of her joints, calibrate her empathy levels until they're exactly where we need them.

I perform a surface-level debugging, but only that; I'm rushing things, and I know it. But I can't help myself. I flip a wall-mounted switch and electricity pours into Vella's doppelganger. It gasps and sputters to life.

"Hello, Vella," I say.

"Father?"

"Yes. Always."

"The Soul Farmer's Daughters" originally appeared in *Metaphorosis*, on 8 February 2019

About the author

Kyle Kirrin lives at 9,000 feet above sea level in Creede, Colorado, where he tends to the needs of two Irish Wolfhounds and writes speculative fiction.

@KyleKirrin

Crying in Public

Madi Giovina

I cry in public parks a lot; we're in the middle of a five-year drought and I want to do my part. It helps, in small amounts, the equivalent of planting herbs in pots on the kitchen counter, or making a vertical garden. My tears are powerful, but I don't have a full grasp on my powers yet. I can't exactly choose *what* I grow or *how much* I cry. All I know is the most I could grow in one crying session was a willow tree—and that was a long cry. But I'm only human, and I can only cry so much. I limit myself to once a day—any more and I wouldn't have a life, and I'd fall into a deep tessellating depression, which would probably generate more tears, but then I'd have most of my crying sessions in therapy instead of in public, and my therapist already has enough plants in her office.

In an average crying session, I grow a baby rose bush or a row of dandelions. Succulents are easy too, because they require less water. And then I can get my friend Frida to propagate them and our impact really multiplies. Even though I'm not totally in control of my powers, I can feel my tears getting stronger every day. This time two years ago, I could barely grow *purslane*. But now, I'm a legend in my small town. (Which isn't saying much, because the legend before me was a kid who was really good at untying knots.)

The community farm asked me to work for them this summer. I said no at first. Even though I'm the best crier I know, I wasn't sure I was good enough to do it full-time, and plus I wasn't sure if crying in the workplace (even if said workplace is a farm) was appropriate. Like I said, I cry in public parks a lot, but that's around *strangers*. I wasn't sure how I felt about crying in front of my boss. I eventually said yes because I needed the money, and I liked that the farm gives away free produce to the community. The lead farmer, Jade, promised me that in exchange for my tears she would teach me about drought-tolerant plants and other farming methods that don't require emotional labor.

My first week, I grew tomatoes, spinach, and basil. About enough for a small salad for a family of seven. Jade was impressed. She had been struggling to grow basil for a while; it was too hot and too dry for any of her plants to survive.

"And you did it just like that! Huh! Maybe I should try crying more."

By my third week on the farm, a strange thing happened: I ran out of things to make me sad enough to cry. Usually when I cried on my own, it came naturally, but now that I was *trying* to cry, I *really* had to try. It was like thinking too hard about breathing, and then forgetting how to breathe. I had used up everything sad in the world, and there was nothing left for me to cry about.

Jade gave me a week off to rest my eyes. I didn't cry at all on my break. My first day back, I grew a lemon tree and everyone clapped. I collapsed from dehydration. Jade made sure to give me plenty of water after that. But a week later, fully hydrated, my tear ducts were blocked again. I tried to cry about not being able to cry, but that only got me one or two tears, enough for a sprig of lavender.

I took my lavender, quit my job, and headed straight to Frida's house. I wanted her to comfort me, and remind me that I hadn't even wanted to work there in the first place, but instead she laughed when she saw me.

"I was wondering when you'd quit." That's all we said about the farm.

We laid in her bed and read *Home & Garden* magazines. I tore out all of the plants I've never grown. Looking at the pile of landscaping photos around me, I realized I wasn't sad about being bad at my job, I was scared I was losing my gift. I dug my face into Frida's pillow and screamed. I must have cried a little bit, too, because when I came up for air, there was a tiny tulip poking out of the pillow in place of a down feather.

Frida plucked it and made me sit on the floor. "I love flowers and all, but please don't make my bed into a garden."

I laughed at Frida standing over me with the smallest tulip I had ever seen that she had just plucked out of her pillow.

"What? I don't want bugs in my room!" she said in her own defense.

That made me laugh more, the idea of Frida's room turning into something out of one of her garden magazines, bees and all. I was laughing so hard, I could feel tears dripping down my face. They cascaded, flowing softly like a lazy river. It felt natural, it felt right; my body was a spring again.

Soon, Frida's floor was covered in a field of aster. The flowers were growing faster than Frida could pick them out of her carpet, so eventually she gave up and joined me in laughing on the floor. That's when it hit me: I could have happy tears too. I kissed Frida goodbye on the head and ran to the farm.

"I want my job back!" I yelled, to no one and everyone.

Jade somehow heard me and came out from the shed, to see me surrounded by a three sisters garden, the result of the runoff of my laughing tears that hadn't dried yet. The sight of me and my gift working again made Jade cry, and I thought I even saw an arugula leaf sprout at her foot. Jade's happiness made me cry more. Soon I had grown a blueberry bush and a row of willow trees. Within a few hours, my crying episode was gossip for the whole town, and I swear since then I've seen more people crying than I have in my whole life. Not everyone's tears grow greenery, but it seems they still spring life.

"Crying in Public" originally appeared in *super / natural: art and fiction for the future*, on 21 November 2019

About the author

Madi Giovina is a fiction writer and the founder of Perennial Press. She edited and contributed to the anthology *super / natural: art and fiction for the future* (2019). Her work can be found in *Bewildering Stories, Down in the Dirt, Raincoat Mag,* and *Penultimate Peanut.* A collection of her short fiction is forthcoming in 2020 on Martian Press.

www.perennial-press.com

The Propagator

Simone Kern

There's a packet of powder taped to my inner thigh, and it feels like the plastic is burning a hole through my leg. Two police officers wave me towards the chem-detecting archway—one last hurdle before I can board the ferry. Sweat pools in the pits of my cooling suit, and my breath comes fast and hot through my respirator. I tell myself they're just city cops, not agents of VerdiCorp. They're just looking for drugs or run-of-the-mill explosives, not the far rarer substance I've stolen. Their arch shouldn't be programmed to catch what I'm carrying.

And it's not.

I pass through without a beep. The cops don't give me a second look. My legs are shaking, but only a small part of that is fear. Lately, whenever I'm near any kind of law enforcement, I see Milo. His tiny body curled on one side, the skin of his face twisted up and back. I see his mouth around the breathing tube, wide with a silent scream, and the gaping hole where the back of his skull should've grown, but didn't.

My blood runs hot with rage. I picture myself pouncing on the bigger cop. Tearing away his air mask. Gouging my fingernails into the soft places of his face.

I am almost getting used to these visions.

I do nothing, of course, but take a steadying breath and force my shaking legs up the gangway. I focus on the feel of the plastic against my thigh. I got away with it. I'm sticking it to the fuckers, in my own way.

Then I'm on board the ferry. A last surge of adrenaline lights up my bloodstream, and suddenly I'm giddy over a crime committed.

The other passengers head inside the purified air of the cabin, eager to shed their bulky outdoor gear. But inside it'll be stuffy and noisy. Every surface—walls, ceiling, seatbacks—will be crowded with the ads I can't bear to see. So I find a spot outside, leaning over the starboard rail. The water slapping the hull is rust-brown, but a strong gulf wind has blown away the usual smog, and the sun gilds each oily wave with a rainbow shimmer.

The ferry pushes away from the docks, carving a path through the labyrinthine chemical refineries towering overhead. The ship channel is choked with rush-hour traffic—gargantuan oil tankers, commuter ferries swapping out day-and-night-shift refinery workers, and the sleek speedboats of executives, darting between us all at breakneck speeds.

We leave the industrial sector behind, smokestacks flaring against the sunset. Winding through sunken neighborhoods, each neon graffiti-scrawled rooftop blazes, like bright flowers sprouting from the murky water. By the time we pass downtown, dusk is falling, and the towers and walkways where the rich live, as high above the waterline as they can afford, glitter against a bruise-colored sky.

High off a close scrape with law enforcement, Houston looks almost beautiful.

Which isn't to say I don't hurt.

I still, always, hurt.

But tonight I'm glad to be watching the stars appear one-by-one in the big Texan sky. I'm glad to see the cube of our habitation block loom up out of the water ahead.

I'm ready to get to work.

Beneath the decontamination showers in the vestibule of our building, I brace myself for the coming onslaught. The hallway and elevator up to our apartment is a gauntlet of triggers. When the last of the polluted water swirls away into the floor, I pull my respirator down and push open the door.

As soon as I step into the hallway, every inch of space—walls, ceiling, floors—bursts to life with ads, designed just for me.

Giggling toddlers wave and run across the walls. They're all the same age Milo would have been.

I unfocus my eyes and hurry forward, trying not to hear. *Time for a toddler-sized stroller? Our air-tight, easy-fold system is lightweight and protects your child from harmful airborne pollutants, like benzene, ozone, metal particulates, and chlorinated hydrocarbons!*

A lot of the ads call my name: *Marisol, buy this! Marisol, you need that!*

But the worst ones are spoken in a toddler's voice:

Mommy, c'n I have a Busy-Bug Indoor Jungle Gym?

Mommy! I want yummy, plant-like snacks from Ponix!

My eyes start to sting. I just have to keep moving. I've tried manually adjusting my ad settings—saying I don't want to see anything with little kids. But every time an ad-scanner catches me out with the stroller, they assume I'm a parent all over again.

The only other ads I get are from VerdiCorp. Every few meters, I get a blessed relief from grinning babies, and the hall is filled with blooming bromeliads and towering *monstera deliciosa* plants instead.

Liven up your living space with VerdiCorp!

Take home a palm, your own slice of paradise. Soil & maintenance included, with no money down, and payments as low as $99.99 a month!

According to the CDC, families with even one plant in the home are 30% less likely to develop cancer. Suicide rates fall for each additional species of plant in a home!

The ad fades as I push the elevator call button, and again I'm surrounded by giggling babies—a toothpaste ad.

As soon as the elevator doors open, I charge in, nearly knocking over our building owner.

"Woah there, Ms. Murphy, what's the hurry?" Rufus chuckles. I slam the doors-closed button. "No little one with you today?"

Like the ad-scanners, he's seen me with the stroller plenty of times, and he's always assumed that beneath the UV-blocking shell, there was a baby inside. I've never felt it wise to correct him.

"Just me," I say, willing the elevator to climb faster.

He leans against the wall and scratches his beard. "Might be some construction going on soon, just a heads-up."

Dread thickens in my stomach. "What's going on?" I try to sound casual.

"Weird thing. Energy bill for the AC keeps going up, even though each apartment's usage is the same. Might be faulty wiring. Thinking about getting an electrician in here to check it out."

My blood's turned to ice. Electricians "checking it out," means poking around in the walls, *behind* the walls, where I'm hiding things far worse than what's in the stolen packet taped to my leg.

"You know Ethan's a journeyman?" I say, in what I hope is a casual tone. "He runs electrical at the plants. I'm sure he could take a look? As a favor?"

"Hey, that'd be great! I like your Ethan. Quiet, but I can tell he's a good guy. Bet he's a good dad too, huh?"

The comment undoes me. Suddenly I'm back in the NICU, watching Ethan hunched over Milo's crib, powerless as me to comfort our dying son.

As soon as the elevator doors open, I mumble a goodbye and bolt for our apartment, past a dozen more squealing toddlers darting across the walls. As soon as I'm inside, I collapse against the door, breathing myself calm in the silence.

The floor of the living area is littered, as always, with the old-timey devices Ethan fixes up for a little extra food money. Analog clocks and desktop computers and mechanical cameras crowd every surface. Ethan sits on the floor in the midst of them, the shape of his back a familiar boulder. He's twisting a screwdriver into the bowels of some dusty, old thing.

"Ethan—Ethan!" I pick my away across the circuit-strewn floor, laying a hand on his shoulder gently. He startles, then pulls one headphone out of his ears.

"Sorry. Just trying to finish this before you got home." He holds up what I now see is a reading light, fitted with a UV bulb. Another grow light for me.

"Thank you," I say, taking the object, although today it sparks more fear than gratitude. "Ethan, I ran into Rufus in the elevator. He's noticed. Says the AC bill keeps going up. He's going to hire an electrician!" My voice is panicked.

"Shit." Ethan rubs a hand down his face.

"I told him you could take a look?" I tug my fingers through my hair. "But maybe we should shut it all down. Dump everything tonight. It's too risky—with this new crop. What the hell was I thinking?"

"No," Ethan cuts me off. He pushes off one knee to stand. Upright, he towers over me. "I'll find Rufus. Tell him it's the smog. It's been affecting power draws over at the plants too. I'll offer to pressure-wash the solar roof. That should help with his bill."

"Are you sure?" I ask, "I mean—about all of it?"

Our eyes meet, and it's a shock. How long has it been since we last held each other's gaze? His eyes seem to have gotten paler—filtered-water-blue.

"I'm sure," he says, pulling me close. He speaks again into my hair, his voice more loving, more decisive than I've heard in a long time.

"Grow your flowers, Marcy."

I used to be terrified of breaking the law, afraid I might do it by accident. When I was eight years old, my school gave us this "Kid's Guide to Texas Law" trivia hologame that I obsessively re-played, memorizing every right answer. As I got older, learned how the world worked—how badly the odds were stacked against folks from habitation blocks like mine—I only became more determined to avoid arrest.

But after Milo, nothing seemed to matter anymore.

Ironically, it was a trip to a prison that sparked my criminal career. It was my first day back at VerdiCorp from bereavement leave, and I was still so sick with grief that I didn't really pay attention to the details when my shift manager explained the job at Sugarland Correctional. I just punched in the order and let the warehouse drones load my boat to capacity, only vaguely registering how massive the order was—20 cubic yards of D-Grade soil, 2000 square feet of Bermuda sod. Grief had robbed me of curiosity. There was only getting through the hours of the work day, earning enough pay so I could bring home something to eat with Ethan. Why I kept going through the motions of this life, and whether I should keep doing it, were questions I couldn't answer.

At the prison docks, my fleet of drones started unloading the cargo and a mustached guard told me I'd be installing a new green space in Cell Block D—Reproductive Crimes.

It was like a sick joke. I'd let Milo suffer to avoid being sent to this place. Now guilt socked me in the gut, solid as a fist, and I struggled to breathe as the guard led me through a series of chem scanners and locked steel doors. My installation drones trundled behind us, hauling the massive bio-storage drums and rolls of sod.

As soon as we passed through the gates of Cell Block D, hundreds of furious eyes from three stories of cells fell upon us, and a howling started up, like the first gusts of a hurricane. The inmates were cursing and wailing, kicking the bars and their beds. Many of them were pregnant—women and trans men. I saw one guy, scraggly beard and swollen belly, must've been nine months along. He was chained to his bed, sobbing into his hands.

The guard leaned towards me, and for a moment I thought he was going to arrest me. Like he also knew what was in my rotten heart. But slowly, I processed what he was shouting over the din. "They thought their little 'protest' would get them something better than that," he pointed back at my drones and their rolls of sod.

We stepped through another set of doors into a blessedly quiet corridor, and his voice dropped to a normal volume. "We meet all the legal requirements. Every inmate gets an hour a day of green time, and we have 1 square foot of lawn for every girl. But that wasn't good enough for them."

We reached a set of steel doors. Above them a sign read: *The Garden.*

"They went on hunger strike. Even the pregnant ones. Wrote up a list of demands—there were like twenty different species of plants on it!" He snorted, swiping his hand over a DNA-reader.

The doors slid open, and we stepped into what used to be a gymnasium—rusting basketball hoops still clung to the walls. But the center of the tile floor had been dug out and replaced with grass—mostly dead now. Huge swaths of brown criss-crossed a few remaining patches of green lawn.

"The warden ordered the medical staff to force-feed the girls. They lost their damn minds over that," he shook his head. "There was a riot, and some of them did this. Got into the cleaning stores and poured bleach all over the grass. I guess they thought we'd replace it with something better," he snorted. "If you ask me, they should lose their green time altogether for this, but the warden says that'll get us into legal trouble. Damn ACLU."

I said nothing, wanting to just finish the job and get the hell out of there. I was still shaken by the inmates' screams. I didn't want to know their stories. I didn't have room in my heart for anyone else's pain.

"Someone needs to sign for the product," I said, passing him my tablet.

"What is this?"

"Terms of your lease," I rattled through the spiel robotically. "VerdiCorp reserves all rights to the living matter. Propagation of plants without a permit is a violation of federal law. Soil is to be used only for growing plants leased through VerdiCorp, and any maintenance, fertilization, or pest control must be contracted through VerdiCorp."

The guard scrawled his signature, then left me alone in the cavernous space. Most of the soil was unsalvageable—poisoned by the dioxin in the bleach. But in the corners of the lawn, the grass was still green. I sent my drones to start digging out all the contaminated soil and called my manager. I asked her what to do about the soil that was still okay.

"All the soil is to be replaced."

"A lot of it is still good."

"They ordered all-new soil, so give them all-new soil."

"I bet there's a cubic yard or more of healthy dirt —"

"Marisol? It's a government contract. All the soil is to be replaced," her tone deepened, barring any future discussion.

"Okay. Got it," I said, hanging up. But I just stared at the pit. The good soil there could provide green space for a hundred families. I couldn't bring myself to order the drones to pack it in with the dioxin-poisoned earth.

I started picturing what could've been done with this space, and with the amount of money the prison had spent on the order. Instead of 2,000 square feet of monotonous lawn, they could've had a slightly smaller tropical garden, complete with trees and vines and flowering plants, and they still would've fallen well within the legal requirements for green space. Was it laziness or cruelty that made the warden order 2,000 square feet of the same damn plant, when he could've just as easily ordered the twenty different species the inmates wanted?

Or maybe he thought he had to punish them for the protest. To control them.

Imprisoned and shackled to their beds. Force-fed and forced to watch their bellies swell. Was it too much to ask that they get to look at some fucking flowers?

And suddenly I understood exactly why they'd poured bleach all over their "garden." Blood pounded hot in my ears, my muscles started to shake, and I felt it too, then. Blood-on-fire, fuck-the-consequences, burn-the-world-down rage.

I wanted to wail like the inmates and kick my drones to pieces. I wanted to find that asshole warden and drive my fingers through the skin of his neck. The clarity and specificity of that vision scared me, but it was also exhilarating. I hadn't felt anything but numbing grief since Milo's death. At least the desire for violence was a *desire*.

But surely I was under surveillance. I couldn't make any sudden movements, let alone enact destruction. I forced myself to take some deep breaths.

And as I watched my drones dig, I realized there was something I could do that would be a fuck-you to Sugarland Correctional, and VerdiCorp, and my bitch of a manager, and even that asshole warden.

I could save the good soil.

Fingers shaking, I programmed my drones to gather up the healthy soil in a separate 200-gallon storage drum from the contaminated earth. My mind raced. What the hell would I do with it? I was supposed head straight from here to WasteWerks, to turn over all the drums of earth. If I showed up back at the warehouse with one drum remaining, my manager would probably fire me just for subverting her authority. I certainly couldn't bring a whole drum of dirt home. I'd have to stash it somewhere.

The soil was the property of VerdiCorp, and even though they didn't want it, were just going to give it to WasteWerks to shore up a barrier island outside the city, that wouldn't matter in a court of law. While in transit, the soil belonged to my employers, and stashing it somewhere was theft.

I was angry enough not to care. I couldn't give these inmates the garden they deserved, but I could steal this soil. I could use it to make things grow.

On the way back to the warehouse, I ran my boat up alongside the third story of a brick mansion in a sunken neighborhood. I had a drone maneuver the drum through a window, shattered long ago. Then I rigged a power surge to flood my drones' charging stations, forcing a reboot that wiped their memories of the entire job. As my boat puttered away through rotting tree-tops, part of me hoped an anarchist gang would find the drum before I returned. I knew already that stolen soil would lead me towards greater crimes, though I couldn't see the shape of them just yet.

When I got home, I told Ethan what I'd done. That I wanted to use the stolen soil to propagate VerdiCorp plants—a federal crime. I'd be putting us both at risk. Was he okay with that?

He looked up from a disemboweled stereo system long enough to shrug and say he didn't care. It was the most we'd talked in days, both of us lost in a grief that made everything seem pointless.

That night I couldn't sleep, and not for the usual reasons. I wandered the apartment, looking for something I could use to transport the soil. The mop-bucket was a good size but didn't have a lid. I needed something airtight, so the soil wouldn't get contaminated by airborne toxins in transit. The Tupperware in the kitchen was too small—transporting the soil that way would take years. Finally, in the back of my closet, I found the perfect thing.

UV-blocking, self-contained air filtration, and it held about a gallon of dirt. It was the fancy stroller Ethan's mom had given us, before we knew. I hadn't had the heart to sell it yet.

So I ventured out just after midnight, loading the stroller into Ethan's dinghy. I was worried I wouldn't be able to find the right house in the darkness, but after puttering around the sunken River Oaks neighborhood, my searchlight fell on a familiar stretch of brick. Inside, I found the drum of soil, untouched. I quickly shoveled a few armfuls of dirt into the stroller, then sealed its beetle-shell lid against the toxic air.

At that time, Ethan and I only had one plant—a neon-green pothos we'd been leasing for years. Its vines wrapped around the walls of the living room, dangling from hooks we'd drilled as supports. That night, I snipped a handful of pothos leaves, just past where they met the vine, and dropped them in water. A few days later, the pothos cuttings had sprouted roots, and I transferred each one to a Tupperware of stolen soil.

From one living thing, many. A theft of VerdiCorp's profits.

Each night for the weeks that followed, I repeated my midnight trip to the sunken neighborhood, hauling about a gallon of soil a night. We started saving food containers for use as growing pots. Ethan scoured the junkyards for light fixtures to turn into grow lamps. Pothos cuttings took over every surface of the kitchen. I loved that profusion of neon green, but if someone were to go in there—Rufus, maybe, snooping while we were at work—it would be obvious we were running a criminal growing operation.

The electric bill had shot up from all the grow lights running 24/7, and our water usage had nearly doubled. One night Ethan asked if I had any plans for what to do with all our new plants, or was I just trying to get us arrested? A fair question, and I didn't have an answer.

The next day, I had off work, and I headed to the city botanical gardens, pushing the stroller, a small razor tucked up in my sleeve. I wanted to see if I could sneak cuttings of some other species of plants.

Beneath the cavernous glass dome of the tropical gardens, the shrieks of countless kids running up and down the paths grated on my ears. The gardens were always jam-packed on Saturdays with families that couldn't afford their own gardens. I was bent over a fire-colored croton plant, trying to work up the courage to sneakily slice off a leaf, when a small body barreled into me, knocking me into the croton.

I slipped a few crushed leaves up my sleeve as I straightened up. A parent rushed over to me, brushing off their kid. "Sorry, sorry! He shouldn't have been running." Both of them had golden-brown skin and long, loose curls.

"No trouble," I said, glad for the chance to sneak a few cuttings. "I think the plant is okay."

"They're so easy when they're little, aren't they?"

"Really? I think they're more finicky. Can't afford to dry out at all, roots aren't established."

She looked at me quizzically, and it took us both a second.

"Oh, you meant...?" I gestured to the stroller.

"Yea. Kids. When they're little, you can just set them down anywhere."

"I was talking about plants."

"I got that," she laughed warmly. There was something about her I instantly liked. A genuineness. Her name was Danni, a teacher.

"Do you have any? Plants?" I asked, gesturing to the croton.

"No, no. We've been saving up for an ivy or something, but with five kids..." she trailed off. "Anyways, that's why we come here so often."

The thought of five kids growing up without a single stem of green at home made me come to a rash decision. My next words would make me something worse than a thief or a propagator in the eyes of the law. I'd be a dealer, subject to minimum sentencing laws of ten years federal prison.

The din of happy children's screams was probably loud enough to obscure my voice from ad scanners, but I whispered anyways.

"You want one?"

A few days after I met Danni, the shower ran cold again, and rather than risk inviting Rufus into the apartment, Ethan decided to fix the plumbing himself. While shining his flashlight back among the pipes, he discovered that above the building's air- and water-recycling ducts, a secret crawlspace ran the length of the building. It was an answer to many of our problems.

Tonight, I take the new grow light Ethan made me into the bathroom and remove the plumbing access panel behind the shower. I squeeze through the narrow opening between the hot water pipe and the wall and push through a curtain of purple-and-green *trandescantia pallida* leaves, emerging into my garden.

The ceiling is only five feet high, so I stoop as I make my way towards the cluttered desk where I do my propagating. Shelves line the walls, loaded with dozens of species of plants, all blazing in the light of a hundred mismatched grow lights. Ethan rigged it so all of them are plugged directly into the power line for the building's AC. We don't pay the bills, Rufus does, and now he's noticed the increase.

After I gave her that first pothos, I told Danni to tell her friends about me. Word spread that there was a lone woman with a black stroller who hung out in the botanical gardens on weekends, who would give some green to any plantless parents. I delivered the plants to their homes directly, tucked inside the stroller. A few times I ran into police checkpoints, but they never asked me to open the UV shield—an absurd bit of luck.

In the homes of my clients, I accepted their lukewarm mugs of Koffee and instructed them in proper plant care. I told them to hide the plants away in a back room, to avoid the suspicion of neighbors. Every time I knocked on a client's door, my heart was in my throat—never knowing whether I'd been set up, whether agents from VerdiCorp were waiting inside with handcuffs.

And then one afternoon, sitting on a bench in the botanical garden, someone approached me who didn't seem to be a parent. No kids in tow. Nose ring, stripe-shaved head, anarchist tattoos crawling up their tanned arms, and spider legs drawn around their sharp-cornered eyes. I had never been approached by a non-parent before. Would I give to one? Was it worth the risk? I was doing this for the kids, right? If I gave to one anarchist punk, how many more would come—

"Marisol?" They sat right next to me.

My heartrate spiked. Besides Danni, I'd been careful never to tell clients my name. "I'm sorry. Do I know you?"

"We have a mutual friend." They raised their eyebrows meaningfully. "Lilith?"

A friend of Lilith's...a friend of Lilith's...the phrase stuck in my mind, like a half-remembered nursery rhyme. It meant something—something high school kids giggled about. Anarchist slang, maybe. I couldn't remember.

"I'm sorry, you have the wrong person," I said, moving to stand.

Their hand clamped over my wrist, their voice urgent. "Lilith knows about Milo. What you *had* to do."

I sank back down, fighting to keep my face impassive.

"Lilith helps people who are...like you were."

Suddenly it clicks. Friend of Lilith. "She's gone to see a friend of Lilith." That's what kids would say when someone met a doctor at a sunken home, late at night, maybe never to emerge. "She tried to visit Lilith." That meant one of our classmates was in the hospital for eating a box of laxatives. Or digging inside themselves with an unbent coat hanger.

They waited for a clump of screaming kids to run by to whisper, "We know you're a grower, and we have something that needs growing. You can help Lilith in her work."

They pressed a twist of paper into my palm and stood abruptly. "We'll be in touch."

I was supposed to feel horrified. I was supposed to flag down the nearest police officer and report them. But I didn't. And by the time I thought to ask, "How do you know I'll help you?" they had already disappeared down the crowded path towards the desert biome.

I peeled back one corner of the paper and peeked. Inside were half-a-dozen tiny, black seeds.

At first, I thought the ultrasound tech was just unfriendly. She slathered cold jelly on my belly, her face set in a grim line. I wanted to chat about names and nesting, but she was all business, pushing the wand vigorously into my flesh. Now, of course, I understand her reserve. With each passing year, she must see more and more pregnancies like mine. To a parent, even a smile from her might seem like a promise she can't keep. The only words I remember her saying were, "I'm going to get the doctor."

Dr. Lavan's eyes were kind and stayed glued to mine when he told us that our baby had a neural tube defect. "A worst-case scenario."

I made him repeat the ugly word, write it down for me, until my tongue could wrap around it, as if that would give me some control: craniorachischisis.

Our baby's neural tube had never closed, would never close, and so both his brain and spinal cord were exposed to the amniotic fluid. No baby born with craniorachischisis had ever survived longer than two days outside the womb.

Dr. Lavan warned me against searching the term on the net. The pictures would be disturbing, he said.

Ethan's hands clamped like vices on my shoulders. I was nearly shouting at Dr. Lavan then, like my protests could change anything. "But I took my prenatals! I've always worn my respirator! Hell, I've tried not to go outside at all!"

"This is just something that happens," he said, so kindly. "It could be genetic. Or you could have been exposed to something years ago. There's nothing to be gained by placing blame."

I could barely get out the next words. "Is he in pain?"

Dr. Lavan paused for too long. "I don't know."

I broke down crying then, knowing it was a lie.

"I've worked with parents in your situation before. This will be hard—for both of you." He turned to Ethan. "I'm going to write you each a prescription for mood stabilizers—"

"Oh, so your ass is covered?" I snapped. "If I lose my mind over the next five months and throw myself—" The warning look on Dr. Lavan's face stopped me, reminded me that every word we said was being recorded, subject to review by life enforcement detectives.

He spoke very slowly. "Given the nature of this pregnancy, it's very important that we do everything possible to maximize your baby's chance of survival. You'll need to be diligent in taking your vitamins, no risky food choices, and be sure not to miss a single check-up."

He didn't need to say the "or else." I knew—if this baby died before birth, we'd both be investigated for evidence of wrongdoing.

He risked his medical license with the next sentence, lingering on two words, letting me know how carefully they were chosen. "I am not a neural tube specialist, but if you were able to...travel...to see a specialist, they might have more...options...for you."

He meant that if we could get North, make it to Illinois, or West to California, there were doctors there who could end the pregnancy.

In that moment, I was furious with him. I had been taught from elementary school to look with horror on the years before *Turner vs. Alabama*. To feel superior to all those lawless, Northern states where the genocide of the unborn continued unabated. And Dr. Lavan knew how badly we wanted this baby. How we'd been trying to conceive for more than a year. I had cried, sitting on the toilet, over a dozen negative pregnancy tests, and I had cried for joy when I'd finally gotten to tell him our good news.

But as soon as we got home from the ultrasound, of course I immediately searched the internet for "chranioarachischisis." I saw the pictures of those tiny, blue-skinned bodies with their gaping skulls, and I knew the shape of agony growing inside me.

And so late that night, holding each other in bed, Ethan and I discussed it. If there was no conceivable way our baby could live, if he was in pain, then maybe Dr. Lavan was right. Maybe we should see a "specialist." But there was no way we could afford the trip across three states, let alone the thousands the procedure would cost. It would be cheaper and closer to get to Mexico, but crossing the border could be deadly. And even if we did somehow raise the money, once it was done, we could never return home, or we'd be arrested the moment we crossed into Texas.

I needed a "friend of Lilith" then, but I didn't know how to find one. I knew there were ways to do it yourself, but I was more likely to kill myself trying. Even searching the internet for answers could get me arrested. And if I wound up at the hospital for any reason, even just food poisoning, I'd face investigation for repro crimes.

So we did nothing. I waited for the long months of my pregnancy to tick by. My symptoms worsened— nausea and cramps and heartburn, aching breasts and back and feet. I was in pain and exhausted all the time. It must feel different, for parents of healthy babies. For me, each day I was pregnant was more miserable than the last. When I couldn't think of a reason to get out of bed anymore, I started taking Dr. Lavan's mood stabilizers.

The baby grew. I tried not to think of him as my son. I tried not to think of him at all. But like any healthy baby, he became impossible to ignore as the months dragged by. I felt his first hiccups, and then his first kicks, but there was no joy in those flutters. I guessed that with each movement, he was writhing in pain.

Sometimes I wanted to claw him out with my fingernails.

Sometimes I wanted to lean over the rail of the ferry and sink to the flooded streets below.

And sometimes, late at night, my lifelong disbelief didn't seem to matter, and I'd curl around my swollen stomach, praying for a miracle. For his skull to grow, for the skin along the back of his spine to knit shut, his face relaxing into a smile.

More often, though, I prayed for him to die. In a spontaneous, painless, medically conclusive way that would absolve me of any wrongdoing.

He didn't, so at 39 weeks, Dr. Lavan was legally obligated to remove him from my body via C-Section, as the baby would have a greater likelihood of surviving that operation than a vaginal birth. Dr. Lavan didn't have a choice in the matter, and neither, of course, did I. The law guided his hand, as he sliced through the flesh of my belly, then my uterus, extricated my mangled child, and reassembled me.

Milo Lopez McMannis (they forced us to name him) lived for forty-three hours after his birth. Nearly a world record. I wasn't allowed to hold him while he was still alive. After, the nurse offered me his corpse, wrapped in a blanket, but I said no. I think Ethan did hold him. I don't remember much, honestly. Dr. Lavan had given me a blessedly strong cocktail of painkillers that let me sleep through most of Milo's life and the days that followed.

Dr. Lavan said we could try again if we liked. That there was a good chance my next baby would be normal. But just in case, I wasn't going to let Ethan so much as kiss my neck after that. He never tried.

I had done what they wanted. I'd been a good girl. I'd thought that if I stayed on the right side of the law, when it was all over, my life would to go back to normal.

But I couldn't turn back into the girl I was before I grew a dying boy, any more than I could erase that mocking scar slashed across my belly.

Two weeks after Milo's death, I was back at work. And I found myself standing in a cell block for reproductive criminals, staring at a mostly-dead lawn.

It took twenty-three days for the mystery seeds to germinate. Of the six, four sprouted into seedlings, and the next time I visited the botanical gardens, Lilith's friend was waiting at my usual bench.

"Seen any interesting plants today?" they asked quietly as I sat down.

"Some kind of plumbago, but I don't know the species. There's no record of it in the database at work."

"I wouldn't go searching the net to find it. You might trip an algorithm."

My guess was correct, then. This particular plumbago must be an abortifacient.

"You expect me to work for you, but I've been thinking. This plant—it couldn't have helped me, right? I was too far along by the time I knew I needed it?"

"Probably," they said. "But your friend Danni? She's the one who told us about you. She needed us a few weeks ago, and we were able to help, because of other growers like you."

I thought of Danni and her husband, five kids already, all of them crammed into an apartment smaller than me and Ethan's. I didn't know how she fed them all as it was.

"I do want to help," I said slowly. "But someone who takes this...they could end up getting sick, right? Even dying?"

"There are no guarantees." They pursed their lips. "But Lilith has many friends. Chemists, doctors, midwives ...going through us is much safer than going it alone."

"Is it in the flowers?"

"The root."

I let out a rush of air. "That'll take time." It'd be another month or two for this batch to flower, another few weeks to produce seeds. At that point I could start a new crop and harvest the four measly roots I'd grown, but who knew if I'd still be a free citizen by then?

Of course, if I could propagate the plumbago from cuttings, rather than seeds—that would greatly speed up my growing times. But plumbago species were tricky to propagate. I would need rooting hormone—a Class A controlled substance. There was plenty of it in the vault at VerdiCorp.

I just had to steal some without getting caught.

The plumbago has just started to blossom, filling the crawlspace with heady perfume. Reaching into my pants, I peel the packet of stolen rooting hormone off my thigh. I grasp a clump of bright white blossoms.

With a sharp scissors, I cut off a leaf cluster just below the node and dip the severed stem in the packet of rooting hormone. I drop the stem in a cup of water, then choose another clump of leaves to amputate.

When I finish, I have twenty new plants. If the roots take, they'll grow much faster than those I started from seed.

Soon, all the pothos, monstera, and kalanchoe I've lovingly cultivated will have to be composted to make room for more plumbago. It'd be too risky to try and distribute so many plants so quickly, and I mean to grow as much as I possibly can.

Lilith's friend said one six-inch root can make four doses. I stare around the crawlspace and do the math, imagining the shelves loaded with white blossoms floor-to-ceiling. My only fear is that I won't stay free long enough to see it. An electrician could bust through the wall and discover my garden. The neighbors might notice the sweet floral smell. Maybe I already got caught on camera, earlier today, slipping that packet of rooting hormone up my sleeve. Or maybe "Lilith's friend" is really a life-enforcement detective, and this whole thing has been a setup.

However it comes, I sense in my bones that time is running out. You can't grow a garden like this in Texas and get away with it forever. Ethan knows it too.

But he said, "Grow your flowers, Marcy."

When I'm caught, I'll be lucky to get life in prison. But fear isn't what keeps me awake each night. It's the wanting to go back in time, to the day I got the diagnosis. I should've chugged a fifth of vodka, hung around crowded places, asking for "Lilith." I should have followed Dr. Lavan home and demanded he give me "options." I should have shown a shred of courage. Tried *something* to end Milo's suffering.

Because the moment I saw him, I knew.

All he did was suffer.

I like to think that when they come for me with handcuffs, I'll hold my head high. That I'll wear a smile when they lead me into the courtroom, strap me to a table for the last breaths of my life.

The world will know, then. I was one of Lilith's friends.

"The Propagator" originally appeared in *Metaphorosis*, on 23 August 2019

About the author

Simone Kern grew up in a small town in Illinois, where they were definitely the only Jewish-atheist-socialist-genderqueer kid in school. After studying creative writing at Oberlin College, they moved to Houston where they taught

English in public schools for ten years. After the birth of their kid, Simone quit teaching to write and be a stay-at-home parent. They love-hate Houston, because their house floods, and it's too hot, and nearby chemical refineries keep exploding, but the people are just too good to leave. Thus, Simone has embraced life as a bayou creature and is busy learning the names of all the Texas wildflowers.

www.simonekernwrites.com, @simone__kern

A Bear, or a Spider, or an Elephant

Edward Ashton

"The night sky is beautiful," Seven says. "Deep and dark, blue-black and starless. It has a certain ineffable purity to it, don't you think?"

Mara glances up. This world is a young one, snugged tight against the galactic core. The stars above her are so fat and bright and crowded together that this can barely be called a proper night at all. She looks back to Seven, one eyebrow raised.

"Not here," he says, his face twisting into a delicate scowl. He's human tonight, mostly, though it seems to Mara that he's gotten some of the proportions wrong. "This night sky is a trollop. I was speaking of home."

Something cries out in the starlit half-dark in a voice like a child's. Seven seems not to notice, but Mara feels a cold shiver run the length of her spine. She leans over to pick a handful of thin branches from the pile she's assembled, snaps the longer ones in half, then drops them onto the fire.

"I envy you," she says. "I barely remember my home."

Seven shrugs, with a rippling motion that betrays an extra joint somewhere in his shoulders.

"Mine was lost long before I found you, but I still recall it in great detail."

The soft breeze dies, and the forest falls silent.

"Found me?" Mara says. Her voice is low and even, but her eyes have narrowed to slits. Seven flinches as if he'd been struck.

"A poor choice of words," he says.

"Was it?"

"The night sky..." Seven begins, but Mara cuts him off with a look.

"To say you *found* something," Mara says, "is to imply that it was lost."

Seven sighs, and seems to shrink into himself.

"I was not lost," Mara says.

"No," Seven says. "You were not lost."

"I was not," Mara says, "not until you *found* me."

"*Found* is the wrong word," Seven says. "I concede it. What word should I use?"

Mara leans forward. The fire casts a monstrous shadow behind her.

"A fine question," she says. "I think *abducted* has a nice ring to it."

She waits for Seven to reply, but he has no answer to this. He never does. This conversation, like all their conversations, is a minor variation on a well-worn theme.

In a literal sense, Mara's accusation is unfair. She did, after all, consent to this. She can't help but feel, though, that consent means little without understanding —and when she consented, she had no hope of understanding *forever*.

To Seven, of course, this is incomprehensible. *Forever* is the water he swims through.

Mara turns away, leans back against her pack and closes her eyes. They're in a clearing of sorts, though this world is covered in great woody ferns rather than honest trees. She should probably set a tent. The ground is soft, though, and the fire is warm. She takes a deep breath in, holds it, then lets it out in a long, slow sigh.

"There is no reason to be sad," Seven says.

"There are infinite reasons to be sad," Mara says. "You should know that better than anyone."

"Untrue," Seven says. "There are tragedies, admittedly, and injustices aplenty. The good are swept under, and the evil prosper. In the end, though, the night sky is beautiful."

"But not this one."

"No," Seven says. "Not this one."

Off in the distance, a creature howls. The sound this time is almost familiar. It could be a wolf, Mara thinks—but no, wolves are far from here, on the opposite side of an unbridgeable gulf in both distance and time. The animals on this planet are built to a different body plan—asymmetric, many-legged, and scaly. She's seen them in the distance, moving sinuously through the ferns, covered in mouths and studded with eyes.

Wolves? No.

But still, they might serve.

Once, on a different world, under a different sky, Mara found the courage to ask Seven if he would ever permit her to die.

"Of course," he said. "Everything dies. You, in fact, will be eaten—by a bear, I believe."

Later, he said, "Well, not a bear, exactly. More like a spider, perhaps? Or an elephant? I'm not entirely clear on the distinctions."

Mara smiled.

"Will you ever die, Seven?"

He stared at her until her smile faltered, then shook his head.

"Nothing is eternal, Mara."

Mara wakes in the early hours. The fire has died, and the glare of the starlight at first tricks her into thinking it must be morning. Seven is curled into a ball on the far side of their little campsite, snoring delicately. She sits up. The forest is laid out around her in sharp-bordered patterns of silver and black. Mara climbs silently to her feet. Seven shifts in his sleep, then tucks his head under one arm like a gangly, featherless bird. Mara turns her back to him, and sets off into the ferns.

In the strictest sense of the term, Mara is free, and always has been. She has walked away from Seven before, sometimes for months, and once for what would have been most of a lifetime if she and Seven had never met. Seven never came for her, and when she finally returned, it was as if she'd never left at all.

For Seven, it may actually have felt that way. His relationship with time is a slippery one, and it has sometimes seemed to Mara that to him, the birth and death of the universe are simply the soft, possibly permeable edges of the space he inhabits. Mara, though, is trapped in linear time, and the thread that stretches from this moment to the one where she and Seven first met is exceedingly long. Her memories of home are fragments, frozen bits of flotsam that have somehow managed to lodge in her brain when the narratives surrounding them have long since washed away. One of those comes to her now—a warmth in her palm, the imprint of a tiny hand clinging to hers. Her eyes fill momentarily. She has to stop walking to wipe them clear.

When she looks up, she finds a dozen eyes looking back at her.

"Well," she whispers. "What have we here?"

The tip of a claw brushes the soft skin below her left eye, trails down along her cheek, then traces the line of her jaw. The creature's movements are silent, but Mara feels the passage of air as its body surrounds her. Cold lips kiss her hand, then her throat. Where they touch, numbness spreads. Her knees buckle. A hundred arms are there to catch her. Teeth nip at the back of her thigh, and she feels a brief stab of pain before that too goes numb. The creature is coiled tight around her now, tight enough that her breath comes short and a rising roar fills her ears. Its mouth covers her own, barbed tongue probing. It...

Stops.

"Mara."

She tries to open her eyes, but she's frozen, pinioned in time, trapped along with the creature, along with the forest, along with...

Everything.

"Mara. This creature is not a bear."

No, she thinks. *It is not a bear.*

"This is not a spider, or an elephant."

No, it is not.

"You mustn't die today."

Seven.

Please.

I'm tired.

"Then rest. We can stay on this world for a while."

You're a god, Seven. Just make yourself a new companion.

Seven hesitates then.

Mara can't recall him ever hesitating before.

"I am not a god, Mara."

Really? What are you then?

"I am..."

Again, the hesitation.

"...alone, if you leave me."

Mara sighs.

I am not made for eternity, Seven.

"There is no eternity, Mara. Patience. In the fullness of time, who can say? There may be a bear."

If she could, she would smile.
Or a spider?
"Yes, or a spider. Or perhaps an elephant?"
Mara holds her silence, but she knows now what her answer will be.
"Mara?"
Promise me, Seven.
"I..."
Seven.
"I promise."

The universe *shifts...*

...and Mara is back again at their little campsite, staring into the coals of their long-dead fire. Seven sits across from her, a hopeful smile on his face.
Off in the distance, the many-eyed creatures howl.

"A Bear, or a Spider, or an Elephant" originally appeared in *Metaphorosis*, on 9 August 2019

About the author

Edward Ashton lives in Rochester, NY with his wife, a variable number of daughters, and an adorably mopey dog named Max. He is the author of the novels *Three Days in April* and *The End of Ordinary*, as well as of several dozen short stories which have appeared in venues ranging from the newsletter of an Italian sausage company to *Escape Pod*, *Analog*, and *Fireside Fiction*.

The Silence of Mother

Gerald Warfield

Bodies floated in the reservoir like tiny islands of gray. Squinting against the morning sun, Moss 17 gripped the back of the bench where he stood and looked out over the water. It was the uniforms that were gray, of course, not the bodies.

This was his customary spot on the far embankment, though he usually came in the evening after his shift at the laundry. Always, he came to this bench. It was weathered and needed paint, and he thought no one else would want to sit there.

Nine. He counted nine bodies, and it had been only three days since Mother had stopped speaking. Couldn't they have held out longer?

On the first day, when Mother didn't wake him, he thought he was being punished. He had committed self-sex for the second time this month, and it was permitted only once. Guilt-stricken, he cowered in his cell until late morning, alternately apologizing and begging forgiveness, but she did not respond. Deciding that he must appear at the laundry or risk further punishment, he put on a fresh uniform, cap, and boots and entered shamefacedly onto the open walkway. At once, he saw something was wrong. In the far lane, two Moss women pulled on opposite sides of a wicker basket. The contents of the basket, tiny breadfruits, lay on the ground. The women, their expressions blank, simply pulled the basket back and forth between them. Already late, he sprinted past them and onto the lane to the laundry.

Breathing heavily, he leapt onto the porch of the squat building and pulled the door open. Great puffs of steam, thick with the smell of soap and disinfectant, engulfed him. Inside, workers bent to their tasks, all except his best friend, Pine 4, whose station was empty.

No one looked up to acknowledge Moss's arrival. Even the supervisor bustled about on her platform without a glance in his direction. Grateful to be ignored, he slipped to his table, took up his hook and basket, and went to fish uniforms from one of the rinse vats.

At his table, he pulled wet uniforms through the wringer while avoiding eye contact with Laurel 9 who worked the same task at the table next to him, and Moss 30 who worked on the other side. Without Mother to relay their words, he could neither greet nor respond. But guarded peeks at the other workers revealed the same wary frowns and darting glances. No one he could see was communicating.

Violette IV dropped her load on the floor. The supervisor, who normally would have scolded her, quickly turned and busied herself with racks of detergent jugs. Wasn't Mother talking to the supervisor?

Moss 17 stopped and straightened. He looked left and right, taking in the whole room. Was it possible Mother was talking to no one? A wave of nausea washed over him, and he leaned on his table. He thought he would vomit.

For the remainder of the day, he worked in a trance. No one stopped for lunch; no one knew when it was. The supervisor glanced repeatedly at a shaft of sunlight streaming from a high window. When it reached the sorting table, she made a show of walking to the door and leaving. Everyone looked at one another and then, without further eye contact, they filed out, separate, solitary figures each to their own cells.

Pine 4 was not at the laundry the next day either. Two Birches were also absent. Gray uniforms went from the rinse vats to the sorting racks, but no one took them to the outside lines. The supervisor arranged and rearranged detergent jugs on her high platform, ignoring everyone on the lower floor. By noon, when there was no more room on the sorting racks, he piled wet uniforms on his table.

That evening, the walk to his cell was interminable. He staggered, not having eaten in two days. A food cart lay parked on the lane near his cell, and he took enough to eat for that night. It felt wrong to eat alone but the confused and furtive faces in the dinner room would be worse.

On the third morning, Pine 4 still had not returned. Other workers were missing, too, even the supervisor. Carts lined the walls and uniforms were being washed in cold water because no fires had been lit beneath the vats. Pine 4's work table in the far corner had completely vanished. Moss pushed his way through the backed-up carts to find it buried beneath a soggy mountain of gray. Appalled, he shoved the pile of uniforms off the table and onto the floor. They landed with a loud slosh. When he looked up, the other workers were staring at him. Ashamed of his display, he fled the laundry.

Pine 4 was special, his best friend assigned to him by Mother when they were still children. Never a day passed that they didn't communicate—until now. He had to know what had happened.

He arrived outside Pine 4's single-cell dwelling breathless, not from the walk, but from the anxiety of leaving work without approval from Mother. It felt wrong, except that *everything* in the last two days felt wrong.

Pine 4's cell, one in a long row of Pine chambers, opened directly onto Pine Lane Two. All the doors were aligned, numbered, and closed save his friend's, which stood ajar. That singularity—although the door was open only a crack—so contrasted with the meticulous conformity of the rest of the lane that it bordered on indecency.

He didn't have permission to enter, but what if Pine lay inside sick or hurt? Without Mother he couldn't call for help. Surely she would understand. Surely Pine would understand. He raised his cap, brushed a quick hand across his smooth scalp, and bit his lip. Then he pushed the door the rest of the way open.

The room lay in shadows, and in the middle, Pine hung by his neck from a rope looped over a lamp hook in the ceiling, his face discolored, his eyes wide.

Moss cried out—inside his head, of course—but Mother didn't hear, and because Mother didn't hear, no one heard.

His pulse throbbed, he couldn't breathe. He wanted to pull the door closed and make the horror go away, but it was too late.

Reluctantly, he crept into the room, stepping around an overturned chair. Pine's cot, neatly made, rested against the far wall. His excretion chair sat on the left, its lid down; the uniform closet on the right stood open. He reached out to Pine's body, felt the coarse material of his trouser leg and the solid flesh beneath. The body swayed in response. He'd not been told to touch Pine, and it seemed a strangely intimate thing to do now, almost erotic.

He dropped his hand, brushing against one of Pine's scuffed, black boots. *Why didn't you wait?* He wiped tears with the palm of his hand. *You always got depressed so easily.* His throat ached. They had shared one another's thoughts, even fantasies since childhood.

Looking up once again at Pine's face, the thought came to him that he should show others that his friend was dead. He glanced about for Pine's green cap, so they would know who he was. It lay against the wall on the other side of the chair. He righted the chair, placed it in front of Pine, and set the cap in the middle of the seat, the "4" facing the door.

For a few moments, he stood before Pine. *Go with Mother,* he thought, and then wondered about the ritual phrase that he had always taken for granted. What did it mean, now that Mother had turned her back on them?

Stepping into the walkway, he blinked and shaded his eyes. Other Pines passed, their numbered green hats bobbing in the morning sun. Standing squarely in the walkway, he looked at the two nearest and raised his hand, extending his fingers toward the door. The first Pine looked into his eyes, slack jawed, and went around him. Moss moved his arm up and down, waving again to the door. The second Pine stopped. Her glance followed his arm out to his hand and then to the cell door. She started toward the door but looked back at him, her brow furrowed, and then she entered the cell. Two other Pines brushed past him from behind and through the doorway. One sank to her knees and hugged herself.

The first Pine stepped back onto the walkway and looked directly at Moss. She extended her arm and waved her hand toward the north, the direction of the reservoir.

He suspected what he might find before he arrived. Those cut off from Mother, and thus from everyone, didn't last long. Once, an Oak had killed a Moss in the field with a hoe. He didn't know why. Only Mother knew, and her punishment was swift. No one could send their thoughts to him; he could send his thoughts to no one. After three days, the man vanished into the woods, probably soon dead.

But now it was different. How could everyone in the village have committed the same crime? And what if some of them didn't know what the crime was? Questions circled and re-circled in his mind. What had happened?

Every day, Mother summoned an individual to attend to her for her nourishment and cleaning. Perhaps the last person called to duty might have seen something or at least know when it happened. But who that person might be, he had no idea. The last time he had been summoned was several months ago, and the memory was dark. Mother was not nice to look upon.

When he reached the reservoir, he could do nothing but stand there, grip the back of the bench and count the bodies. Never had he needed a command from Mother more than now. When animals drowned in the reservoir—anything from a rat to a farm animal— someone was sent to remove them lest they make the water bad. If he could report these bodies to Mother, he was sure that she would tell him the same. The mere thought of her instruction was enough to start his feet toward the muddy bank.

But he stopped before reaching the water. Iris 9 was approaching the reservoir. Surely, she had not come to drown herself, too. He looked away, hoping not to attract her attention. In the corner of his eye he saw her sit down on the next bench, which relieved him, and he ventured another glance. Her eyes were closed; her brow was knit. Was she in pain?

Oddly, she did not have on her purple cap— another sign of their collective descent into chaos—but he recognized her without it. Did she remember? She was even sitting at the same bench as before. But perhaps, like others, she had no thoughts at all in the absence of Mother.

The incident had occurred more than a year ago. One of Mother's mistakes, yet his cheeks burned to think about it. In the evening, after work, he had sat by the reservoir on this same bench, and a woman had sat at the other end. He couldn't see the number on the front of her cap, but it was purple, so he knew she was an Iris. She faced forward, watching a pair of ducks on the shore, but in a sidelong glance he saw her smooth neck and the subtle blush of her cheek. *May I touch you?* he asked. Mother did not relay the Iris's answer, but then Mother was sometimes slow. *And if Mother is willing, may I kiss you?*

The Iris still showed no visible response, but he heard the voice that Mother conveyed back to him. *I would touch you, too. Kiss me.*

He took a deep breath and faced her. Reaching out, he took her shoulders and leaned forward to kiss her lips. The young woman twisted away violently and leapt up striking his nose with her elbow and tumbling him to the ground. Her eyes were wide, and her mouth gaped open as she looked down at him.

Moss was too confused to call for Mother. He felt blood trickle from his nose and reached into his uniform for a cloth. Just then a man, another Moss, walked stiffly from the lake. Beyond him, on the next bench, sat another Iris, a 9 on her purple cap. Moss and the other Iris looked at one another, Moss now holding the cloth to his nose to stanch the blood. She put her hand to her mouth, and they fled in opposite directions.

He turned back to the water and took a tentative step. Mud squished beneath his boot. Surely she was watching. A few more steps and cold water poured over the tops of his boots, chilling his feet. She probably thought he had decided to drown himself like the others.

The nearest body floated facedown. It seemed to be male. From the green of the cap, still on his head, it was another Pine. Wading until he was waist deep, Moss could not bring himself to touch the body, so he reached around and gripped the back of its collar.

He towed the body until it touched the mud in the shallows, and then it was harder to pull. Another pair of hands reached down and grasped a trouser leg. Shocked at the intimacy, Moss's reaction was to look away. But the hands pulled with him, and together they dragged the limp body to the edge of the water and through the mud, leaving long ruts up to the dry bank.

When he straightened and dared to glance at her, he saw that her right arm was injured. Four long gashes, recent wounds, had scabbed over. They had not been treated, no salves, no bandage, and there was a bit of red along the perimeter of each. The sleeve of her uniform was also ripped. It was as if an animal had clawed her. Moss turned his head so as not to intrude. He wanted to ask her for help with the rest of the bodies, but of course, Mother wasn't listening.

When he entered the water again, he was gratified that she followed. Together they dragged the remaining bodies onto the bank, lining them along the edge of the grass. To give them a more orderly appearance, they straightened the arms and legs. It helped, making them tidy.

Winded, he sloshed in his wet boots and uniform to his bench and sat, shuddering from the cold. Iris followed and sat at the other end, which pleased him, although it also made him anxious. Was she following commands? Did she hear Mother's voice? He emptied his boots of water. Was he supposed to do something? Finally, he became so self-conscious that he stood to leave, but when he stepped forward his boot caught the bottom edge of the bench and he fell, pitching forward onto the grass. Stunned, he lay facedown, little flashes of light wiggling before his eyes.

Hands gripped his shoulder and turned him over. Iris knelt next to him, and he looked up into her face. She had touched him. Should they mate now? But in her eyes he saw the same haunted look as he had seen on the faces of others. No, this had nothing to do with mating. She struggled with the absence of Mother, just as he did, perhaps more so. He got up and clumsily tried to brush off the front of his uniform.

He didn't want to leave Iris looking so troubled. On her own, she had helped him pull the bodies from the reservoir, and she had touched him. Emboldened, he stepped closer and took her hand. She did not respond.

From habit he cried for Mother. How was he to know what to do? People were dying around him, and now he held Iris's hand.

Cold despair curled in Moss's gut. He could not talk to Iris, and she could not talk to him. They simply stood, holding hands.

His original idea, to find out Mother's caregiver of three days ago, seemed hopeless. There was nothing to do except—perhaps—maybe—*to go see* Mother. The thought made his knees weak. Yet the hand he held gave him courage.

He motioned with his arm and fingers like he had done before, but Iris did not respond. He started forward, and her hand slipped out of his. No, he couldn't do it alone. Reaching down and taking her hand once more, he gently tugged, and this time she moved forward to walk with him.

On Central Lane, they passed ominous signs: the jacket of a uniform crumpled on the ground, a single shoe resting in a doorway. Near Pine's street, a vulture tore at something unidentifiable beneath a tree. Moss grimaced, and they both hurried forward. He had never before seen a vulture in the village. Just the fact that Iris walked in the open without her numbered hat signaled a growing disorder. How could people communicate with her if they didn't know her number and that she was an Iris?

Coming to Lane One, they rounded the corner, and ahead of them a wide roof of thatch spread above the round house that sheltered Mother. Iris jerked to a stop as if only now realizing where they were going.

What should he do? Should he try to pull Iris along with him? Should he leave her and see Mother by himself? Moss looked back at the imposing house of Mother and then at the sky, searching for answers. Mounds of clouds stacked overhead, pressing down like enormous rolls of fat. A cold wind had sprung up, and he shivered. His uniform was still wet from the waist down. He saw that Iris shivered, too.

Urgently, he pulled on Iris's hand again. She looked wild-eyed but allowed him to lead her toward the structure. He smiled, trying to convey that he understood. The presence of Mother could be—difficult. There were cases where people had fainted upon seeing her for the first time.

The House of Mother was different from any other house in the village. It was round and covered by a vast thatch roof. A central portal framed in heavy wooden beams led to two access passages, one left and one right, both of which circled to the far side of the structure and to the entrance of Mother's chamber.

As they entered the portal, Iris slumped as if she might sink to the floor, clearly overwhelmed by the sheer peril of entering into the Presence without a summons. Moss supported her with an arm around her waist, but his own heart beat wildly, too. He resolved then to protect her from any punishment. He would tell Mother that it was not Iris's fault, that she was merely weak and had allowed him to lead her into this perilous breach of protocol.

Inside the hallways of Mother's house, ceramic lanterns always burned on high shelves, even during the day. It was each caregiver's duty to fill the lamps and trim the wicks. But now only a single lantern sputtered to the left of the doorway, its open flame casting a fitful light into the perimeter passageway. Moss squeezed Iris's hand and called out in his mind one last time asking permission to enter into Mother's presence—to no response.

Moss released Iris's hand and reached up to take the remaining lantern from the shelf. Together, they started down the left passageway, their footsteps rustling the straw on the floor. As they got closer, a buzzing could be heard from the interior. Iris squeezed her eyes shut so that Moss had to lead her. They rounded the edge of the passageway and entered into Mother's chamber.

Moss raised the lantern. Additional light streamed from a circular opening above. In the middle of the room the mountain of flesh that was Mother rested on a circular platform of wood raised the height of a man. Great swaths of cloth draped the massive mounds and hung limply off long rolls of fat. Her head at the top, dwarfed by the gargantuan body, lay back and faced upward. Her mouth gaped open. Diminutive arms hung limp, seemingly from beneath her massive jowls. The hands, more like claws, terminated in pointed nails.

Below the heavy platform that supported Mother, a thick layer of straw had been stacked to catch the waste that fell from her massive body. Clotted and thick with flies, it clearly had not been changed.

Paralyzed at first, Moss gaped. As shocking as the great, ruined body was, the presence of vultures was worse. Perched on ledges of fat, they had torn through the cloth to gouge out chunks of flesh with their hooked beaks. A long strip of flesh dangled from the beak of one.

Some of the birds spread their wings and squawked at the intrusion of Moss and Iris, but others simply continued their feast. To the right, a wooden stairway and a long plank extended out over Mother so her feeders could reach her mouth. Feeding bowls were stacked at the bottom of the stairs, some of them still full.

Moss let out a cry. Crouching, he placed the lantern on the floor and then bounded upright and ran to the stairs, leaping them three at a time. Reckless, he charged out onto the runway above Mother, waving his arms and crying out again.

The vultures squawked and flapped into the air. Two circled the room beneath the roof; the rest exited through the opening in the center. Moss stopped at the end of the plank, suddenly frightened at what he had done. He had cried aloud, and that was shocking enough, but now he looked directly down into Mother's face. The end of a feeding stick rose from her mouth, but not far enough. Now it was clear what had happened. He knew how long the stick was. It had been crammed down Mother's throat.

He could not read an expression on her face. Flies covered her eyes, and her mouth was filled with squirming, white maggots. The gorge rose from his stomach, and he swallowed to keep from throwing up. Sinking to his knees on the plank, he gripped its edges, suddenly fearful of losing his balance and falling onto the great, decaying body.

The humming of flies filled his ears. The odor, pungent and rotten, threatened to choke him. And then he saw that she held things in her delicate, clawed hands. In one, a torn piece of gray cloth was stuck in her claws. In the other she held a cap, a purple cap.

Who had done this thing? Frightened, yet determined to find out, he lay prostrate on the plank and reached down. Leaning perilously over the side of the runway, he could barely reach the cap. Careful not the touch the flesh, he lifted it from Mother's limp fingers. But, already, he knew what it said. Kneeling on the runway, he turned the cap right-side up. The number "9" was embroidered on the front.

His eyes clouded, and he dropped the hat. He hadn't meant to. It hit the plank with a little thud and then bounced off to fall into one of the gaping holes the vultures had excavated, too far down for him to reach.

Trembling, he looked back at Iris, so small, standing just inside the doorway. She stooped, picked up the lantern by its handle and held it out to him, a lonely, desperate gesture. She tried to smile, but it came out a grimace.

Moss looked back and forth between Iris, holding the flickering light, and the massive, putrefied body below. How could she have done this?

He turned on the narrow runway and attempted the hazardous walk back to the stairs. Certain he would fall, he spread his arms for balance. The stench had grown in power, threatening to knock him from the narrow gangplank. Would he lose his balance and fall into the mountain of rotting flesh? He did not fall. He reached the steps, gasped for breath, and descended the stairs to the dirt floor.

Iris had remained in the same spot and followed his progress with a somber face. Again, she extended the lantern, tears streaming from her eyes.

When he reached her, he didn't know what to do. This woman, alone, had done the unthinkable, causing a profound turmoil from which there would be no recovery. She deserved his wrath, but it was a different emotion that rose within him, something he had no name for: admiration perhaps, though far stronger, more like yearning to be with her, to keep her close to him.

Iris weakened further as she endeavored to hold the lantern. Lips trembling, she struggled, opened her mouth, and abruptly made a sound. "Ka."

It meant something. Yet whatever it was, she continued to diminish like a distant light fading out. She lowered the lantern further. She was giving up. Moss could feel it.

He, too, struggled to make his mouth work. "Ka." The sound was similar to hers. Then he reached out and clasped the lantern. Their hands touched. He would help her. It was a desire that overrode all others. He wanted it more than he feared Mother or the village.

Moss looked back at the monstrous body resting on its framework of timbers. Iris's great work was unfinished. One final thing remained to end the era of Mother, and he would do it. Iris would see him do it.

With the lamp, he went to the edge of the heavy platform that supported Mother and to the mounds of hay and detritus that lay beneath. Kneeling, he took off his hat and placed it on the top of the mass of dry stems and leaves. Then, he raised some of the brittle tangle from the floor and placed the lantern beneath it. The hay sucked the fire into its dry thicket with a crackling sound. Moss rose and turned away. He did not want to see the flames take his hat.

When they reached the outer doorway, Moss hesitated before stepping into the sunlight. Iris moved close, so close their shoulders touched. He looked down to see the four deep scratches on her arm where her uniform was torn. They seemed to be healing. He wanted them to heal. Glancing about the edge of the village, no one was in sight. They must leave this place before the flames were noticed. "Ka," he said.

They walked quickly and without holding hands, so as to attract little attention. When they passed the last row of cell houses on the west side of the village, they came to the fields where crop plants were tall and bread pods ripe. Several villagers harvested amongst the furrows, picking the pods and placing them in long sacks. They could not have been told to do so. It was a good sign.

At the far end of the field on a low rise stood one of the huts where they had been instructed to keep tools with which to work the crops. The hut drew them, and they followed one of the long furrows between the tall breadfruit plants toward the isolated structure.

A few wooden diggers and a basket were propped against the outside wall. The thatch was in good repair, and the inside, full of tools, could be emptied. There would be room enough for two cots. Moss had never heard of two villagers living together in the same cell. Mother had never commanded it, but the thought entered his mind. It was part of a bigger thought that he hadn't put together yet of the two of them together.

He made the sound "Ka." She came to his side and put her arm around his waist. Looking out through the doorway, they saw a white column of smoke rising from the village. It pointed into the sky—a sky where the clouds had broken and begun to drift away.

"The Silence of Mother" originally appeared in *Score – an SFF symphony*, on 2 March 2019

About the author

Most of his adult life, Gerald Warfield lived in New York City, on the upper west side and in Chelsea. His first job was at the Library and Museum of the Performing Arts at Lincoln Center. He marched in the first Gay Pride Parade in 1970. After leaving music, he supported himself writing how-to books in finance, and textbooks in music; his formal education was in music theory and composition (UNT and Princeton). He's an old man now and lives in a small Texas town where he's very out of place. He was accepted into and survived the Odyssey Writers' Workshop in 2010. That's where he really learned to write.

www.geraldwarfield.com

The Color of My Home is Red Like an Apple

Evan Marcroft

The color of my home is red like an apple. That is what God told the father of all my fathers, who told all their daughters, who told me. I do not know what an apple is, only that it is sweet and red like my home. My name is Anan. I have lived as long as nine suns, and I have always served God.

When I was a baby, my father was chosen to be Nurse of God. As expected, he involved me in all the procedures of pleasing God. Every day, my clutchmates and I were brought before Him to play in the sand, for God delights in the happiness of children. When we grew older we were allowed outside the village to spearfish along the river where our mwku'oh cattle drink. The fat of scuttlefish, when rendered, made good oil with which to polish God's body, and their shells were fitting gifts for children to give.

I have seen nine suns live and die now, and it has since become my duty to help clean God. This morning, as every morning, we five chosen gather outside my family's house and walk together behind my father to the great tent where God lives. My father says that when He came to live with us my people had no village, but wandered after the mwku'oh with our homes rolled up upon our sledges.

Today the daggerwind rages, blasting the village with the desert's glass dust, and so the panels of His house are tied shut. We enter only with my father's permission, bent low in respect.

Inside we find that God has written a greeting in the sand for us. *Hello to you, my children,* he says. *I hope that all of you are well this day.* We knuckle dutifully and begin our work. Nananqi and her sister Wocamhsh scrub clean the wrinkles of His old feet, while Tsuvuyé shines His one huge eye. Yonweh, with her small hands, brushes out the crevices of his body. I alone have the prized task of polishing the golden wings through which God drinks the light. My friends smolder with envy, but I am the daughter of the Nurse, and so it is my right. God never said I could not be proud.

Sweeping my fingers across the glittering planes of God's wings, I can feel the captured fire crackling within. Not even from His own welcome do I feel more blessed than in these moments. His body is stronger than bone and stone. Through drought and famine, storm and stagnation, God will be with us. With me.

When we are finished God scrawls His thanks with His one protracting arm. The characters for *gratitude, smile, to you,* toned by a precise inclination of His eye. *Know, children, that I appreciate you all,* God says, and my hearts bake in his warmth. There was a time when He first came to live with us when none of this was understood. But in His patience He taught my people to make sounds with shapes and so learn to commune with Him. Everything we Hhmuadi have, we owe to him. It was he who taught us to sculpt river mud into houses that could withstand the daggerwind's wroth, and to fashion that wild glass into windows. It was He who tutored us in the natural hierarchy of men and women so that we would no longer live in our incorrect way.

As always, we pray to Him before we go, knuckles to our hearts, for the strength of our crops and for the fullness of the river, for a path to the Blue Star after death.

Sometimes God replies. This time He does not.

Outside God's home, the village is bustling. The daggerwind has calmed, and the earth glitters like clear water. Families are rolling up the thick glass-catching cloaks on their houses to let in the light. The wives are heading to the field to reap needlecane. I spy a group of young men entering from the eastern gate with a dead wraraqwa on a sledge behind them. The ferocious cactus-beast is a full twenty hands long, and still bloated with the blood of its last meal. It will make a fine addition to tomorrow's feast.

All Hmuadi have their work to do before then, and I am no exception. Women's chores keep me busy throughout the day. There are mwku'oh to bleed for nectar, water to pull from the river and boil. When the sun begins to settle into the claws of the Mimirtaigh Mountains, I go with the women to ready tomorrow's feast, stripping the sweet fruit from venomous needlecane by mazarine twilight and then by firelight. No matter how hard I am worked I do not complain—not now, not ever before. I accept the role that God has given me, both its blessings and its burdens. Neither do I cheat or steal, or strike others in anger. I should not fear to be chosen come tomorrow.

Nevertheless, when I at last crawl into my rootthread bedding, my stomach churns as though worm-ridden. So much rides upon such a small span of time. Tomorrow, those of us children who have lived as long as nine suns will gather before God to receive his blessing—to be chosen. After that, I will be a woman in full, ready to marry and make sons and daughters of my own. And when I die God will send me to the Blue Star, to live with my ancestors along the florid banks of a river free of illness and pain.

I should not worry. I know I am virtuous. But still, sleep comes slowly. There is a long day between now and then.

My hearts beat along to the frantic rhythm of the Choosing Song. I have witnessed this rite many times from the amongst the crowd, and though I dreamed of the day I myself would stand here at the door God's house, at the cusp of womanhood, somehow I never understood the reality of it, the soon-ness of it.

There are thirteen of us who will now be as old as ten suns. We kneel on the raked dirt outside God's house in stoic silence, in contrast to the revelry around us. I watch the young men regale spellbound children with the tale of yesterday's hunt, pantomiming the wraraqwa's snarling death. My own brother Mangiirse, the tallest and strongest, leads his friends in a drunken hunting hymn.

I remember how proudly he went to God at his Becoming two suns past, already a brave hunter. I have nothing to be proud of but my obedience. I wonder if I will be able hold my head as high. I wonder, quietly, if my obedience will be enough.

Finally, but long after my legs have gone numb, my father emerges from the crowd and raises his hands, hushing the village. Behind him, I can see men hoisting the windows of God's house. The silence deepens as his holy body comes into view. In this place he has resided since he arrived from across the Sea of Stars. How great a God he is, to surrender heaven and live contentedly among us like an old grandfather.

My father beckons to the boy closest him. All the boys will go before the girls, no matter that I am the daughter of God's Nurse. So it has always been. My father leads the boy into God's house. It is hard to see, but I know what happens. A happy murmur ripples through the crowd.

I realize soon that my faster wishes to save me for last. The other eleven children go by in what seems like seconds. All are chosen, all are flung into the embrace of the crowd to be met as new men and women, beloved strangers. Finally my father reaches for me, and I come unsteadily to his waiting hand.

I have been in the presence of God more times than I can count, yet kneeling before Him now, it feels as though I am beholding Him for the first time. I know rationally that he is not much taller than me, but from down here He seems a monolith. His body gleams like a geode, His surfaces smooth as ice and indestructible as the world itself. His fathomless eye swivels and fixates upon me. What does God think about, I wonder. What could trouble a mind as great as His?

His arm pivots towards me, the joints of His complex hand whirring softly. It hangs over me like a fate. My breath catches in my chest. I hover at the invisible seam between past and future, where one person ends and another begins.

I clench my eyes shut. I wait for His touch.

And it does not come.

In my head I stretch the moment as long as I can, giving it chance after chance, until I am forced to open my eyes. The hand of God trembles above me as if gripped by something unseen. The lens of his eye dilates and contracts at random. I do not so much hear the horror spreading through the crowd as feel it, a blistering chill upon my back.

My people are realizing slowly that my future has come, and I am not one of them.

My father's hand closes around my shoulder, and a sudden, saw-toothed wail tears its way out of my throat. I rear up, thrashing away from him. He recoils as one would from a snapping beast. Fear uglies his face. Fear of *me*. The red earth beneath me teeters like a plate balanced on a stone. I run for my home, and the gathered village parts for me as though I am diseased.

I am to be exiled.

The deliberations were short. I am not the first to be refused by God, and nothing should be different because I am the daughter of his Nurse. I am no longer Hhmuadi, and so the obligations of kinship are not owed to me. No man will condescend to marry me, and even if I am raped, any children I might bear would be tsöach matat—refused from birth. As a girl-woman with no use, I and my possible offspring would pose a drain on the village's resources. But more than that, I am abhorrent in the eye of God. My former people will not suffer me to pain him with my presence.

Of course I must go. I can respect the logic.

But still, it hurts. Like a death that does not end.

At sunrise the morning after my refusal, my father rouses me from my bed of blankets and leads me to the edge of the village. My father provides me with a heavy cloak, a bundle of provisions, a horn of water, and a lavaglass knife. There is sadness in my father's eyes, but resolution in his jaw. I am to walk in a straight line to the East, into the desert, and never return.

I do not get far before the thought of my family breaks me and I come running back. If I can just see their faces one last time, take them fresh into the desert with me, then everything will be alright. I promise that I won't mind dying. I know that he will understand. He is still my father.

I do not take six steps before a stone from his sling catches me in the leg, and I crumble into the sand.

This time he and another man gag me and carry me far out into the desert. This time, when he lets me go, I see in his expression that the next stone will find my eye. The last I will ever see of my father is his determination to kill me.

The time, I walk as I am told until when I look back all I see behind me is a plane of red sand and powdered glass cut into two infinite halves by my hoofprints. Within hours, that umbilicus will be blown away by the wind, and nothing will connect be to my home but the aching hollow in me molded to its shape. I fall to my knees where I am and wait for the desert to take me. I do not cry; I am somewhere far past that.

The fickle desert does not take me, and so I continue toward that uncertain place where it will. An empty day passes before I find shelter beneath an overlapping of stone slabs, and stagger into the hollow beneath to faint. Swaddled in my cloak, I somehow I survive the hateful cold of the night, and in the morning I plan the direction I will go to die.

The desert continues uninterrupted into the east further than my knowledge of the land extends. Far to the south is the Sharp Ocean, a whorl of glass knives taller than ten men standing end on end, whose reaches have yet to be explored by my people. There is no life there, no water, no respite from the sun. Surely it would kill me. But to the north are the Mimirtaigh Mountains, forbidden to my people by God since a day long forgotten. It is said that to be caught in their shadow is to be hidden from God's love. Thinking on it, I find the old taboos no longer feel so dire. And I am forsaken already.

I walk for what seems like the lifespan of a hundred suns. I had never understood how vast the desert was. When you are young, the world is only as big across as the furthest thing away you know of. But the world does not care what you know. My rations and water do not last long. I starve and thirst until I stumble upon a dried-up oasis and lap up the last of its muddy water. I find a few small, hardy fruits in the sand and stay the night. The next day I am forced to scurry up a heap of rock to escape a stampede of wild mwku'oh, lest I be chewed to slurry under their threshing cilia. Another day, I am given only minutes to burrow under the ground by the howl of a nearby Thirsting Tree. I try not to choke on sand and powdered glass as the towering monster lumbers over my hiding place, snuffling after the scent of moisture.

But in between these frenetic moments is nothing. Burning nothing. Freezing nothing. I almost welcome the danger when it comes.

I try, and fail, to not think of my family.

Sand eventually gives way to dirt. Little by little, the mountains rise up beneath me like pregnant bellies. As night falls and their shadow inches over me, I feel no more cursed than before. I do not know what kinds of beasts make the mountains their home, so I do not know what to fear. The trek is no easier or more difficult than it was through the desert, only steeper. I suck sour water from pools I find in bowls of rock. I gnaw roots and look for more when they don't kill me. I sleep in the cracks between great stony teeth, and wonder when the world will think to scrape me loose.

It does not take long. On my third evening in the mountains, dark clouds begin to dew on the glass of the sky. I am quick to abandon hours of forward progress to scuttle back to a cave I know is safe; I reach shelter moments before the storm hits like a hammer. It is the wind's wailing that nearly kills me; it masks the howl of something else.

I do not hear the Thirsting Tree until it is upon me.

I have no time to react, and nowhere to run, as the narrow cave mouth is invaded by a thicket of grasping tentacles. My leg is enveloped immediately and numbed by the monster's venom. I am ripped from the mountainside like a dagger from a sheath. Frigid rain pelts me as a dangle over the monster's canopy. Its clawed roots grip the rock above my hiding place, a spearfisher perched to harpoon. I watch a flower-shaped mouth bloom amidst its writhing boughs—the face of so many Hhmuadi nightmares—and unspool dozens of spear-tipped tongues.

I do cry then, because I am only ten suns old and never became a woman.

But I also grope for the knife at my hip and, curling towards my feet, slash it through the Tree's boneless hand. Its scream defeats all other sounds; the pressure on my leg disappears. I squeeze my eyes shut, expecting a painful fall. Instead there is a light that pierces my eyelids, and a sound like a beaten drum as wide as a village. Something hits me hard in the side, and the next I know I am tumbling end over end down a muddy slope. I glimpse the Thirsting Tree teetering far above me, blazing like a torch. Then my head strikes a protruding stone, and I cease to think.

Some time later I awake. It is still storming, and I am still hurting. I lie in mud, at the bottom of a gorge. Beside me is the body of the Thirsting Tree, split down the middle and smoldering noisomely. In that struggling light I make out another figure. A single, crooked arm. A flat black eye. Outflung wings, in which flecks of gold glisten.

God watches me die.

I stir at something clanking. I sit up out my bed of mud and look around for the sound. The awareness that I am alive flitters unobtrusively through my head. The sun is out again, and I can see clearly that God is there, no further than thirty hoofspans away. He is drumming statically on His back for no reason that I can see other than to get my attention. For a moment I swoon with rage. God, who has never moved from His house in generations, has come all this way to mock me in my suffering. But there is something about Him that chills me almost simultaneously.

The God I knew was pristine white and silver. This God is utterly caked in earth, and where His body is exposed, I see now that it is a dull red like the earth of this world. I creep cautiously closer. My God's feet were lovingly cared-for; the plates of this God's feet have come unraveled and sunk into the ground, as if He has stood here for a hundred suns. And on my God's chest, where He had worn a square of red, white, and blue stripes, He now wears one that is all red with a speckling of gold stars.

This is not my God, I realize. This is a different God altogether.

He stops tapping on himself as I approach Him as I would a wounded animal, staying well out of reach of His hand. I do not trust this God to be as gentle as my own. His eye swivels haltingly to fix on me; I can see that He is nearly blind with clinging filth. Over the course of a minute, He laboriously scratches something into the hard mud in front of Him; intrusive plants infest the joints of His arm. I squint to read His message. *Do not be afraid.* The same first words my God ever wrote that my people understood.

"Are you... God?" I ask. I have to be sure.

He writes the negative symbol. *No.*

Before I can reply, He begins to scrape out something else. *You Hhmuadi,* He says, after much effort. *You come from place where God is, yes? Us hope to see you for long time.* This not-God speaks his own language poorly. His grammar is full of holes. He uses the symbol for 'us' when He should say 'me.' *If you come see me later than now, this tool may die waiting.*

"Why did you never move from this spot?" I ask.

This tool broken on landing. I can see Him struggling to articulate himself. His diction is the simplest possible. *Am immobile.*

"Where did you come from?" I must wait for Him to brush away old words before He can draw new ones.

We provide this tool from place called Blue Star.

I frown. "You look like God, and you come from the Blue Star," I say, "But you say you are not God, and you call yourself a tool. I am sorry—I do not understand."

The symbols for me, name, question. *What is your name?*

"Anan," I answer, uneasily.

Hello Anan. You are able to call us Morning Star. We are sorry, but your God lied to you.

I sit cross-legged before Morning Star, no longer fearful of him, because he is too old and broken to hurt me. He has listened to my story, and I now I will listen to his.

His writing is less ponderous now that I have washed the sand from his joints and pulled out most of the weeds. *To begin,* he says, *the Blue Star is not a paradise. Hhmuadi do not go there when they die. It is a world like this one, but very far away. You could live one thousand times and never walk there. It is not a place of joy and plenty. There is as much death as there is here. There is even more death than there is here, for there are many more people.*

"But you said there are no Hhmuadi there."

Another kind of people live there. They look very different from you. You would think them monsters if you saw them.

"How many are there?" I ask, challengingly.

I wait as Morning Star inscribes a number, and then adds degrees of multiplication to that number, until he exceeds the limits of what is possible. I scoff at the absurdity of it, a number so large it has no name.

The Blue Star must be carpeted in people as thickly as the desert is carpeted in grains of sand.

I tell only the truth, Anan, Morning Star chides. *And it was they who sent me here a long time ago, as they sent your God here even longer before that. You must understand that your God and I are not living things as you are. We are a kind of tool. We are masks-that-walk, mindless as dirt. The people of the Blue Star could not come here themselves, so they sent these tools to see through. To live through.*

"That does not make any sense," I sneer. "No-one can make a tool that walks and speaks like a person. How can a tool love the way God does?"

The people of the Blue Star are very clever, Anan. We know many secrets of the universe that you Hhmuadi do not. We make sledges that float in the sky. We have weapons that can knock down mountains. You cannot even dream of what is possible for us.

"Us?" I ask, and in the very next moment, I coldly understand. I think of the loretellers of my village who through magic-seeming trickery can throw their voice wherever they like, sometimes even into another's mouth. I think of the yeyemocawh, the Laughing Hole, that mouthsome predator who sings the songs of other animals to lure prey into its warren.

Yes, says Morning Star, observing the change in my expression. *You are speaking with us right now, through this tool. There are many of us present, instructing the tool what to say. Just as there are many others telling your God what to say.*

"That's not true," I snap without meaning to. My face is growing hot. My hearts begin rail like captives against the cage of my chest. "You're lying."

If that thing is God, then what am I? Morning Star makes a sympathetic gesture with his eye. *We understand your doubts. You fear what it would mean if it were true. You fear that it was not divine will that ruled your life, but instead the whim of mere people hidden behind a curtain. You fear that you worshipped something no greater than yourself. You fear that you were cast out from your family for no good reason. But you told us you have always been virtuous, and we trust you. So why would God reject you unless it did not matter to him?*

"Why?" I demand, shooting to my feet. "If that is all true, what would they deceive my people for, and why for so long?" I am too heated to catch myself saying *them* instead of *Him*.

It was not their intention. They sent their mask here to study your world, to know the Hhmuadi. But your people met saw their mask and called it God. They of the Blue Star decided it would be easier to let them believe that. You might not have cooperated otherwise.

My life, and the lives of my family, those of my ancestors, whose hearts all cleaved so dearly to God's wisdom—all just pretend games. All of us, led along from birth to death by nothing more than a hand puppet. Of course I fear that be to be true. I flinch from the notion as I would from something venomous. But for all my want, I do not know the words to argue.

Even now I am compelled to defend God against these evil words. He was as much as father to me as the man who sired me. It was God who raised my soul, if not my body. But I try and try and still cannot see the logic in damning me to die in the desert when all I have for Him is love. My tongue is prone beneath a thousand excuses, each as light and thin as shed skin.

They say that God knows what lies down paths unseen. But I do not have his eyes.

Morning Star steps into the silence I leave him. *We of the Blue Star are not one tribe like you are. We are two, and we have fought for a very long time. At first, there were too many of us for our world to provide for everyone so we had to fight for food and water and land. Now there is little left to fight for, and we fight because we hate each other. It was the enemy tribe who sent the mask you call God to your world. They wanted to know if it were possible to travel there and take your food and water and land. They wanted to condition you for their arrival in the future. We could not let them be the only ones on your world, and so we sent our own mask—this mask. When they make one spear, we make two. When they make ten arrows, we make one hundred. That is the way of our world.*

"You must want the same thing, then," I say, miserably. "You want to take our world to feed your own. If your mask had not broken, we would worship you instead."

Most likely. Your world hangs like an apple among the stars.

I snort a surprised and unhappy laugh. "You should lie about something like that."

Why would we? We have stopped our enemies from setting out for your world many times. Not for your sake, but simply to spite them. They have done the same to us. Many believe we may already be out of time. That the apple is out of reach. So we have no reason to lie to you.

"Then what were you waiting for all this time?"

We have told you the truth you would never have learned otherwise. Now we ask that you do something for us. He scribbles something more. The symbols for 'return,' 'home,' 'destroy—'

Go back to your village and destroy God.

The first word to find its way back to my stunned lips is, "Why?"

This tool will soon break. We do not want our enemy to be the only presence on your world. If not us, then no-one. That is all.

"No," I say, "No, no, I can't do that."

What do you owe it?

My family, my home, everything I love, one half of me declares. The other half whispers, *everything that was taken.* "I can't just believe you," I say pleadingly. "You tell me that all I know is a lie. How can I know that is not a lie as well? You are no better than God, to tell me what is real with no proof." If there is a real world then let me stand upon it, I silently demand, or I will forget you for a fever dream and continue on to where I die.

Morning Star raises his hand to bid me be quiet. *A fair complaint, Anan. There is a rock behind you. Go and bring it to us. With it, we will prove the truth of all we have told you.*

I glance back at the dun-red stone he speaks of and go to pry it from the ground. It is no easy task, for I am withered from my slog through the desert. A thousand crawling things skitter out from underneath it as I roll it into my hands. The earth-chilled mass of it threatens to pull me over as I lug it back to Morning Star. Swung by a larger man, its sharp spine would cave through a head like a fist through an egg.

I return to find Morning Star with his neck bent, his eye downturned. His arm is tautly horizontal. He has left one final message for me scrimshawed into the ground.

This tool cannot move properly. It will soon cease to function entirely. It has no further use to us but this. Let it become the proof that you require.

The stone you hold is the fruit of knowledge.

Swing it hard.

I stare at the words for an endless time. And then I raise the rock above my head.

At night, my village is as silent as any other patch of the desert. I creep beneath windowsills, silent as an illness, walking on my hands when necessary. I have padded my hooves with a poultice of resin and grass to mute my footsteps.

I do not linger near my family's house unnecessarily, though I long with both hearts to peer inside and see how my family has changed in the time I have been gone. To see if my baby sister has grown her teeth, if Mangiirse has earned the starglass hero-knife he always coveted. Perhaps they have not changed at all. They have not been through the desert as I have.

Never more clearly have I beheld God's influence on my village, the invisible scaffolding of His tutelage standing around my house, articulating its dimensions, constraining its possibilities. Our laws are given, our roles assigned, our language taught. I cannot imagine what we might have become if God had never come.

A teacher is both the giver and keeper of knowledge. For every good thing he gave us, there must be a thousand things he withheld. A thousand paths along which my people might have walked. Without him we might wander the desert still, desperately chasing food and water. But with him we cannot help but camp in his light.

With him, we wander nowhere.

Only one man keeps watch outside the House of God. It is his solemn duty to sleep in the day and guard God at night. Rather than face his brawn and lavaglass club, I wait until his patrol around the House takes him out of sight, and then slip inside from the rear.

God's form slowly resolves from the darkness like an animal imperfectly camouflaged. I hold my breath and wait for any sign that He is awake. I wave my hand before His eye to see if He will stir.

"Can you hear me?" I whisper, as loudly as I dare. "Please, God. Tell me you are real," I can't help but ask of him. "I need you."

And even now, it is true.

Even now, I crave His absolute world. How could I not? All the happiness I ever knew was in the fist of a greater power. We Hhmuadi are not the product of our own will, and even now I could die with that, so long as I could believe it meant something.

"Tell me that you're real." I beg to be saved from the unknowable wilds of a godless future, for my world to be clutched like a sweet, red apple, so long as it is held with love. "Tell me I am wrong. Just tell me. Please."

I wait, but I receive no answer, and I know that it is not refusal. Whether He is God or the mask of one, he is simply not there.

Perhaps it is night on the Blue Star.

I undo the sling I wear across my shoulder and cup in my hands the jag of rock that I painstakingly carried here from the mountains, across a gulf of sand and time.

I must be efficient, for the guard is close by. There is no hesitance in me; my faith has never been stronger than in this moment. I am without doubt that the great truth of God could never be shattered by just a girl with a stone.

"The Color of My Home is Red Like an Apple" originally appeared in
Metaphorosis, on 29 March 2019

About the author

Evan Marcroft is a half-blind yeti-person with a sideways foot and an allergy to the sun. When he was a child he dreamed of writing important works of Earth-shaking beauty and settled for writing fantasy and science fiction instead. He currently lives in Chicago with a cat and a loving wife who foolishly believes he'll someday make real money doing this. You can find his other works at *Pseudopod, Strange Horizons*, and *Metaphorosis*. You can reach him on Twitter at @Evan_Marcroft and contact him for any reason at Evanmarcroft@hotmail.com.

There is a City, He Told Me

Evan James Sheldon

There is a city where the outer walls shift and entrances dance away, so that a passerby might think they are merely approaching from the wrong side. If you know about this city, if you are patient and cunning, you can find a way in, and what a city! Its interior is not flashy, not filled with magicians and trees burning with inner fire, but there is comfort there you can find with diligence and pursuit. People leave, as they will, and the inhabitants wait longingly for those travelers to return, for the simple joy of conversing with someone else who understands the city's intricacies.

I can see my father forming the words, and it is not yet a struggle. His patchy steel-wool beard parts right before he says each phrase, like his own body knows what he is going to say. I haven't heard of these cities in years and they've changed during my time away, they are different cities now. Maybe his purpose is less veiled. Maybe my understanding of what he speaks, his intent, has deepened, but either way tonight, I understand his meaning.

His hands shake. But his voice does not waver. It is strong, mellifluous, golden, and sweetened by the red-and-white-striped peppermint candies that clack against his teeth as he speaks, providing a counterpoint rhythm to his cadence. I had forgotten about the candy.

There is a city where the young people paint their teeth black so that it looks as if they have no teeth at all. They guffaw and toss bits of food at the elderly, taunting and smacking their lips. This practice continued until one child painted their teeth gold. Now they turn their faces, their mockery, to the sun. The very old lounge in the shade of tall trees while the faces of the young burn to a crisp, tongues wagging.

His words come slower, still clear but plodding. I pull the blanket up and tuck it beneath his beard. It is the same color, a rough steely wool, and it looks as if his beard extends to the floor, pooling there. I wonder how long he has sat in the chair by the fire, waiting for me. I wonder if he can see the darkening of foreign suns on my cheeks and forehead.

There is a city that moves, that picks up shop and will relocate to a new place on a whim. The inhabitants believe it is not the city that has moved, but the rest of the world. That the earth beneath their feet has shifted through no fault of their own. They come to believe in a conspiracy of geography and leave markers, carvings to indicate locations they know.

He believes that these places are real. You can tell by the tenor in his voice, his fervor, the way his cloudy eyes remain on my face. He knows these places. He thinks about the inhabitants. That girl who ran across the muddy lane wearing only one shoe. That couple who drifted in and out of traffic, oblivious to the sirens, to the honk and bustle of the city. That woman who painted her body to match the sky and stood frozen in the square, reduced to an outline, a shimmering against the clouds.

Maybe they are real, conjured by his retelling. Maybe they have always been real, and I have just been searching when I should have been understanding.

There is a city where the ghosts never leave. They stay. They linger. The city's inhabitants push through transparent faces and fingers like a permanent fog. The living have become used to the lingering ghosts, and paint their houses with bright, vibrant colors to find their way. The living paint their faces in elaborate designs to see one another smile. The living laugh and move through life unencumbered by those that have come before them. In the ghost's desire to stay, they have in fact, become invisible.

When he stops speaking I hold up my hand to his mouth. There is warmth there and breath still. He is afraid, but even now, he will only speak of cities. What can I say to assure him that I won't forget? I form the words, but they feel flat, inadequate on my tongue. I stoke the fire and wait.

There is a city made and sustained only by songs sung by children and no one is ever left alone in silence.

There was a time when I would not have waited. There was a time when I was off visiting my own cities, searching to see if what he said was true. I wonder now whom he told of these places in my absence, or if they bottled inside of him, waiting for me and only me, to spill out when I returned.

There is a city where they only decorate in bleached bones of their fathers, a celebration, a homage.

Or if he has been speaking slowly, continually, trying to call me back.

There is a city where rain bursts from the ground and all the trees twist roots into the sky, where a person might walk right into the heavens.

There is a city that everyone visits, but never returns from.

There is a city…
There is a city…
There is a city…

This time when he stops, I know he is done. I hold my hand to his mouth and there is no movement. He is finally quiet. I linger for a moment, in the firelight his beard and his blanket shine like hammered metal.

When I get home, my daughter rushes into my arms. I am grateful for the rain to hide my tears, but she is too smart, too quick. But she doesn't say anything when she lays her head on my chest. We sit by the fire and listen to it crackle. *Did you know, little one, that there is a city where an old man grew a metal beard? He always sat by a fire that never dies. And the words he spoke were false, but he never lied. And when his time came, his son wrapped him up tight in the metal that grew from his face so he would be warm for his journey. Because he could no longer stay.*

Why couldn't he stay? she asks.

Because he had new cities to see, a hundred hundred new places to visit.

She is quiet, but her eyes grow wide, and in the light of my own fire, they shine like living ore.

"There is a City, He Told Me" originally appeared in *Metaphorosis*, on 30 August 2019

About the author

Evan James Sheldon is a Senior Editor for F(r)iction and the Editorial Director for Brink Literacy Project.

evanjamessheldon.com, @EvanJamesSheld1

As An Absence

Joanna Michal Hoyt

"Something quieter," Liane said. Her earclip switched from the shuddering cries of the skaboom station to soft crooning. "Get the next book from the Classics Reading Challenge," she told her screen.

"A squat grey building of only thirty-four stories...." the book began. The sentence was haloed, which meant someone on her preferred discussion channels had commented on it. She tapped the sentence.

Krptn: U notice all the dystos start urban

>Astro @ Krptn: not animal farm

>>Krptn @ Astro: thats kid stuff not real dysto

>>>Aeaeae @ Krptn: They think you can push anything on kids if you add cute talking animals. Animal Farm and Watership Down, depressing politics; Bambi, depressing theology...

>>>>Astro @ Aeaeae: get a life

>>>>>Mika @ Aeaeae: ad hominem

>>>>>>Astro @ Mika: chick thinks shes writing book we want 2 read

>>>>>>>Aeaeae @ Astro: check your gender assumptions

"Gender assumptions" was haloed. Liane tapped.

Two hours later, halfway through a podcast about charges against the director of a film on the history of cross-dressing, an ad for the Cultural Classics Reading Challenge flashed across the screen. Liane swore. "Get me back to the Cultural Classic," she said.

The screen obliged. "A squat grey building of only thirty-four stories..."

She'd taken the CCR Challenge to read thirty-five stories in the year; took it partly to impress Brian; had meant to keep on to show she had never cared about impressing him...

Kendall's avatar flashed in the margin of the screen.

>u bored 2?

>>just distracted

>>>give it up that thing's so old

>>>>stop hating on everything old where'd western civilization come from

>>>>>where u think wes civ's going

By the time she'd answered Kendall, argued with June about whether she'd been mean to Kendall, and ignored Max's remarks about what a bitch June was, it was close to midnight. Liane put the reader to sleep. She couldn't seem to get herself to sleep.

She'd read three Cultural Classics in six months, and she couldn't remember how the last one had ended. She knew she'd gotten to the end; she had the completion badge on her SeeMe avatar; Casia had congratulated her, Julie had said something mean about how slowly she was progressing... Julie, who had seemed so understanding about Brian, but was now on her block list... But might Julie be saying mean things about her now? Things she couldn't see because...

Liane stood in front of a squat grey building of thirty-four stories. It looked derelict, the windows boarded up. She needed to see what was inside. As she approached she saw the windows were covered with fiber optic screens, not boards. The screens flashed, telling her in dozens of colors and hundreds of fonts to

KEEP MOVING. Every screen was different. Every message was the same.

Another flat thing in the wall didn't flash at her approach. It sat there dully, ignoring her. It didn't look like a smartdoor, but...

She swiped her hand across its surface to wake it up. It didn't wake. It did, however, quiver under her hand. There was a sort of lip she could grab, an edge raised above the level of the wall. She pulled.

It was a dumb door like the ones on the cheap old apartments. It didn't obviously scan her thumbprint; it just swung open.

It gave onto a wall of fluttering paper with words printed all over it, very large. She read the words at her eye level: "Each of them carried a notebook in which, whenever the great man spoke, he desperately scribbled..."

For a moment she imagined them, whoever they were, with those big retro computers, dictating frantically. But they wouldn't have to do that if the great man was talking...

Not dictated. Scribbled. An old word. She'd heard it before. One day when she was two, the power and the interweb connection went down. Her earclip fell silent. She screamed. Her grandmother brought out a pad of drawing paper and crayons and let Liane make marks all over those white pages, marks that did not go away when she swiped her hand across them.

"Let her scribble," Gran said.

So. The frantic men were marking up paperbooks. She was standing in front of a giant paperbook now. Dull things, paperbooks, completely uninteractive, nobody used them anymore, but she'd seen people reading them in historical films. Reading them as if they were actually interested.

A voice spoke on the other side of the paper. A cultured, self-mocking voice, with something desperate underneath.

"He manifests himself as an absence," the voice said. "As though he weren't there at all."

"Who's absent?" she tried to ask. She couldn't speak. She couldn't breathe, either. *She couldn't breathe...*

As she woke, gasping, her earclip repeated softly, "It was just a dream. You're all right. Nothing will hurt you. You are perfectly safe. It was just a dream."

"Shut up!" she shouted, throwing her earclip against the wall. "I really wanted to know!"

The earclip alarm woke her from across the room.

"Shut up," she said.

"Do you need help recovering from your Mood Event?"

"I'm not having a Mood Event!"

But of course the earclip had sent out a Mood Alert to her contact list. Her older sister Jeanette had sent seventeen nagging messages, one of which might have been appropriate twelve years ago when Liane was thirteen. June said Kendall would surely understand if she apologized to him now and explained she was feeling unstable...

Liane deleted all her personal messages from the last twelve hours. She answered the work messages asking whether she needed someone else to cover her shift as a HuMart cashier (HuMart advertised the Human Touch and pointed out that a personal interaction including a greeting and a smile reduced the body's production of cortisol hormones by 46% for a three-hour period, thus leading to approximately 22 hours of increased life expectancy) or her daily assignment for SciOpMag (Liane was one of their human Content Generators, and she'd invented the statistic about greetings, smiles and cortisol). She informed both that she could work. Before her HuMart shift she had fifteen minutes to unwind on Webplay…

Webplay offered her tranquility-inducing guided meditations; when she disappeared them (and told the hoverbot which asked why, "Because they make me want to puke,") it offered some first-person shooter games for stress relief. "I am not a psychopath!" Liane snarled at the screen. "Get me the book."

She read the sentence about the thirty-four stories again. A soft ping announced a Challenge Partner message. "Finished Chapter 1!" Stacia said. "God what a totally horrible society."

Who was Stacia? Liane couldn't remember.

"Yeah, horrible," she muttered, looking back at the central column of text.

"Makes you glad we don't live in a time when people imagine things like that," Stacia persisted.

Liane deactivated the conversation, read about the cold light in a room which appeared warm only on the yellow microscopes where it glowed "streak after luscious streak in long recession down the work tables."

The word *recession* was haloed. Tapping it, Liane saw Mika's link to an article forecasting another Great Recession. Liane signed a petition to prevent the crisis through regulation; told June the petition was not a libtard idea; donated five credits to boost the petition; wished she hadn't; read half an article on how to avoid impulse donating before an alert reminded her that it was past time for her to leave for HuMart.

She smiled and greeted people for eight everlasting hours, wondering if a bit more yellow in the decor would make HuMart feel luscious instead of sappy, and if that would just encourage people to linger so you had to smile longer at them. Her face hurt from smiling. Last week she'd spun seventeen versions of an article on how smiling caused deep body relaxation. She could write a searing rebuttal under a different name…. She planned to do that at the end of her shift. Instead, as she swayed on the commutrain, she asked her screen, "Who reads paperbooks?"

Several biospots on mass murderers noted that they were antisocial types who read paperbooks. Liane wrote a SciOp piece on Socially Secured Sanity, then went back to her query.

The exciteweb offered several articles recommended by her contacts. June had liked the piece on liberal elitists who shut themselves off from the views of Real Americans by reading paperbooks instead of electreading and the one on lazy liberal moochers who freeloaded by reading paperbooks, parasitically sucking in other people's words without contributing anything of their own. (Liane was halfway through completing their survey on productivity when she realized this was an unproductive use of her time.) Max had liked one about conservatives wanting to drag humanity back to the age when there was nothing to read but paperbooks written by dead white men. (Liane spent ten minutes reading arguments about whether a certain memoir had actually been dictated by a dead white man after his death, and, if so, whether or not this should be counted as a work by a member of an underrepresented group.) Stacia had commented on one saying conservatives who were too intellectually limited to appreciate intertextuality accommodated their puny brains by reading static paperbooks.

Liane was halfway through writing an infojolt citing all four articles when she realized that every reader was guaranteed to find at least one of them offensive. She swore aloud when she realized this, forgetting to turn the soundshare off, so Kendall thought she had sworn at him, and when she explained that she was thinking about work and hadn't actually heard what he was saying about his breakup with Kaitlyn he wasn't any happier. Liane shut off the convo. Blanked the screen. Turned her head. One of her fellow commuters was very rudely looking, not at his screen, but at her screen. Or her face? In any case, butting in. She lifted her device to photograph him. He ducked his head apologetically. "Get me back the book," Liane told her device. She read almost half a screenful of text before the CommuterAlert flashed to tell her she'd reached her stop.

Back home, she wrote half a lackluster rebuttal to the smile article, and a whole piece about the stress-elevating effect of being looked at by strangers, in between deleting angry messages from Kendall and nagging messages from Jeannette. "My head aches," she muttered. "Go away!" she snarled at the ad for an Electronic Long-Distance Reiki Head Massage for Only 14 Credits. She looked away from the screen before she could see it asking her about another Mood Event.

Something twitched in her peripheral vision.

A piece of paper had been shoved under her door. *Come to the Library* was scribbled on it.

Liane stared at it. Then at her door. Messages weren't supposed to come in analog. A drone couldn't have gotten that thong under her door, could it? And if a person had...People didn't just go to each other's doors. Not without sending an InviteMeIn notification.

Maybe the man from the commutrain was stalking her. Maybe if she stepped outside he'd hit her over the head and...Only it would have made more sense if he hit her before she went inside. Why wait out there and shove the paper in?

Maybe there was anthrax on the paper. She'd seen an old movie about that.

She'd already picked it up. She thought of searching for information about how to tell whether you'd been poisoned by an unexpected piece of paper. Then she thought about the ads she'd certainly get from hazmat companies, and the mandated visit she'd probably get from hazmat inspectors. Then she thought about being arrested and tested for paranoia. Then she decided if she'd been poisoned it was already too late.

There were smaller scribbles on the back. *The Library is on Green Street, half a mile past the Eighteenth Street crossing. There's a statue of a heron at the end of the driveway. Come at any time, day or night. The door's not locked.*

Only a real idiot would follow directions like those, Liane thought as she slipped on walking shoes. Only an idiot would go out alone to meet some...stalker? kidnapper? lunatic? she told herself as she locked the door behind her. Only an idiot would obey scribbled instructions from a total stranger, she told herself as she turned onto Green Street.

"What you doing?" Max buzzed in her ear.

"Lying down," she subvocalized back. "Flu. Going to watch something mindless, relax."

"Best show:..."

"Bye," she said, seeing the stone heron looking at her from the side of the road. This must be the place...

"Something calming," she subvoed to the earclip as she turned off the road and started up the long driveway. "Keep the volume low."

No answer. Didn't it know what she found calming? "That piano stuff," she subvoed. The silence continued. "Say something," she said aloud.

Her earclip was silent. A lilting voice from the shrubbery said, "Hello."

Liane screamed, turned to run, tripped, fell heavily.

"All right," the voice said mildly. "I'm just going to get that branch out from between your feet, then I'll back off again. There's no interweb signal here."

"Who are you?" Liane demanded, rising awkwardly so she could look down at the small dark woman who had greeted her.

"Luisa," the woman said. "One of the night librarians. Will you come in and try a book before you go?"

"I've tried books," Liane said sadly. "I'm on month six and book four of the CCR Challenge." She frowned. "On the first page of book four," she admitted. "Since last night."

"If you'd like to read more, you might want to try reading in the Library."

"What kind of rewards program do you have for reading there?" The CCR Challenge gave out badges, and also a chance to enter a drawing for…she'd forgotten what, but it had sounded exciting.

"None. People read here because they want to read. If you don't want to read, you can go home."

Kidnappers, Liane thought, would promise something exciting, not just let her walk away.

"Okay, I'll try," she muttered ungraciously. Then, remembering, "If my signal's off, I can't get the book."

"What book?"

Liane frowned. "I forget the name. It's a Classic. There's a grey building with only thirty-four stories…"

"Brave New World. We have it." The librarian started back up the drive.

"Why were you down here?"

"I came out to look at the moon. The people in the story I'm reading had been doing that."

Liane craned her neck to look up. In movies the moon was round, but the only big thing shining in the sky that wasn't obviously man-made was a blobby just-over-half-circle. "Is there something wrong with the moon?" she asked.

"Not that I can see," Luisa said.

"But the shape… Isn't part of it missing?"

"Waxing gibbous," the Librarian said. "You can't see all of it because of the earth's shadow, but it's still there."

He manifests himself as an absence, the voice from Liane's dream said as she followed the Librarian up the curving driveway. The trees along the driveway flashed like screensavers as a breeze flipped them toward and away from the moonlight. Liane went to snap a video; remembered she couldn't. Kept going.

The Librarian showed her to a screenless little room with three tatty chairs in the middle and paperbooks on shelves all around the walls. She handed one paperbook to Liane. The cover showed a guy staring at a movie-shaped moon with a lot of scribbles over it. Liane tapped the scribbles but they didn't move or flash. She opened the pages (remembering the paper wall in her dream), read again about the squat building, the yellow streaks, the scribblers. She paused to flip to the back. One hundred and seventy-seven pages; it was going to take forever....

She sighed, turned the page, and made herself read on. Stopped, staring at the page. They were growing people in labs, as if people were things? Aeaeae would say...

She couldn't see what Aeaeae would say now. She kept reading, horrified. She wasn't so much reading words now as standing in that terrible building and listening, listening, while the people around her scribbled and smiled as though nothing was wrong...

The words came back to her again at the description of some rose petals: *pale with the posthumous whiteness of marble...* Like the weird moon out there, she thought. Once again there was no one with whom to share the observation. Lacking that, she went out onto the porch to look at the moon again.

The Librarian met her coming back in. "All well?"

"Yes, but I want to make a note, and my EPad's not working here either."

The Librarian held out a paper notebook like the ones the eager boys in Chapter One had used and a little analog pen that made a blue ink mark on Liane's hand when she took it by the point.

An hour after that Liane had scribbled several fragments of the book.

"Most human beings have an almost infinite capacity for taking things for granted."

"Words can be like X-rays, if you use them properly —they'll go through anything. You read and you're pierced."

"Wouldn't you like to be free to be happy in some other way?"

But the story kept grabbing her by the throat and making her forget the words. That poor man Bernard, wanting something he couldn't even imagine but wanting it so badly that it made him hate everything he did have... she could understand that. And John. John Savage. He didn't make any sense and he didn't make any sense and then—when he was staring at Lenina, wanting her as desperately as he ever had and hating himself for wanting her once he knew how much she disgusted him—

She remembered Brian with a sudden wrench. Seeing herself smiling from his photowall, seeing all the Likes. Smiling into the camera's eye with him. Waking up in the small hours, seeing his screen lying on the blanket between them, his hand just an inch from it; pressing the keypad to his thumb; and seeing, and seeing the HotOrNot entry he'd made about her. The photos he posted—The first one wasn't bad, but her hair wasn't right; the second was pretty good, but she hadn't meant it to go on the web. And under "Most expensive thing she ever bought you" he'd listed some crummy meal, not the game night she'd paid for... and under "Crackup Quotes" he put nothing, nothing at all..

She might not have minded that either if the Re-Viewers hadn't ranked her as deeply Not-Hot. She might not even have minded that so much if she hadn't recognized two of the R-Vs as her cousin and her friend...

And she looked back at Brian, the light from the screen casting a strangely angled silver light over the planes of his face, and he was just as beautiful as ever. And she wanted ... she wanted...

She winced at the pain in her mouth. She must have bitten her tongue. She couldn't even post another angry message on DumpHimNow and be reassured by likes and bracingly infuriated by mean remarks. Couldn't even tell her earclip, "Distract me." Everybody was absent. Everything.

All she had was the book. She threw herself in...

An hour after that the Librarian came back to find Liane curled around the book, weeping.

"Are you all right?"

"He shouldn't have died like that! They shouldn't have lived like that! None of it should have been like that! And I don't know why people want to read if it makes them feel like this."

"You'd rather be happy? Busy and happy and not interested in stories?" The Librarian's tone was neutral, but her glance was sharp. Liane opened her mouth. Shut it. Looked back at the book. "No," she said softly. "They shouldn't have lived like that. I shouldn't either. I don't want to stay absent."

The Librarian gave Liane a smile that lit her dark face. "How do you want to live?"

"I don't know. Do you have a book about that?"

"I have several thousand books with ideas about that."

"Same thing as the convo rooms, then. Nobody agrees."

"Likely not. But here you might have time at least to figure out what you mean. What you want. What you hope for."

Liane opened her mouth. Shut it. Thought. The Librarian didn't seem to be in a hurry now. She waited as though silence was normal, was unthreatening.

"I hope so," Liane said.

"As An Absence" originally appeared in *New Orbit*, on 1 June 2019

About the author

Joanna Michal Hoyt lives with her family on a farm/intentional community in upstate NY where she spends her days tending goats, gardens, and guests. Part of the community's aim is to encourage people to tale time to be less distracted; despite this, Joanna sympathizes strongly with Liane's hopeless distraction. In the evenings Joanna reads and writes odd stories, some of which have appeared in magazines including *Mysterion, Daily Science Fiction*, and *New Orbit* (where this story, and an accompanying editorial, initially appeared in June 2019).

joannamichalhoyt.com

A Layer Thin As Breath

Thea Boodhoo

"Valley. Can you still hear me?"

Julian's voice filtered through her dying radio. The *Prince of Cats* was a speck of light, dimming through the gold-grey film that, atom by atom, was devouring her helmet.

Valley tried to say something, anything. Failed.

Julian was sobbing on the other end. "I'm so sorry. I'm so, so kzzzzzzchchchcffft—" and that was it. Her radio was gone.

"Oh god," she breathed to herself, to no one. "Oh god," *I don't want to die. I don't want to die.* She sobbed once, twice, and then, with tears pooling in her eyes and the *Prince of Cats* invisible through the liquid, she found a pocket of calm, like stepping from a noisy bar onto a cool, quiet street.

Something brushed against her hand, and she cried out, startled. Her vision was still blurred by tears, and the thing dissolving her space suit was like an iridescent veil across the glass of her helmet, but through it all she could see the outline of her hand.

Not her glove.

Her hand.

The veil, delicate as a cobweb when it had floated innocuously through space, was finally at the layer of her skin. It felt like cool air at first, then like nothing. Then her fingernails tickled.

She was so surprised to see her bare hand, covered only in iridescent gauze, against the black of space, without the sensation of it freezing solid, that she forgot she was dying.

When she remembered, she screamed again. And as she screamed, the iridescent veil dissolved the final layer of her helmet glass and fell toward her face.

Hyperventilating, she felt it against her nose and forehead, cheeks and lips, like cold mist, and every time her breath sucked in, the thing moved further into her mouth. She tried to spit it out, but in it came, in and in and in, forcing past her coughing and gagging, pushing into her nose and ears, and–

And she could see again. It had absorbed her tears.

Her spacesuit was gone.

She was still alive.

Her scalp itched. She touched her head — her hair was gone, and her fingertips felt strangely sensitive, on the edge of pain. She looked at her hands — her fingernails were almost gone. The itching faded, and she felt the cobweb against every centimeter of her skin, enveloping her like water. It squeezed. It squeezed everywhere until she could barely breathe — and then released the moment before panic overtook her again.

It was in her eyes, but it didn't resist as she blinked.

Her eyelashes were gone.

It wrapped around her teeth and tongue, against the roof of her mouth and the inside of her cheeks. She tried to swallow, and felt it lining her esophagus.

Nausea overcame her. She dry heaved until the feeling faded.

She floated through space, holding her knees and crying tears that were immediately absorbed, breathing without drawing air into her lungs, the spidersilk feel of the space thing that enveloped her like impossibly thin gloves between the skin of her hands, which should be frozen, and her shins, which should also be frozen.

The cobweb had penetrated every part of her. It had eaten every strand of hair and every fingernail and toenail. She was left with nothing else, like a forgotten mannequin in a dusty storeroom.

She realized she was in shock. But she wasn't dead. She felt her toes and squeezed one where there should have been a toenail. It hurt.

Ok. It hurt. *Ok. I really am alive.*

Valley dreamed of all the ways this could have been avoided, tracing back the sequence of events all the way to her first fossil hunting trip with her parents when she was five. She cursed them for it. Then cried again. She put the memory away. *No. You've taken everything else, you can't have that.*

Valley had still been working on her PhD when she and Julian found the first fossil. It was a small mystery, like a crumpled piece of laundry with a too-regular microtexture, on a Kuiper Belt meteorite on Titan. When the press release came out, tech billionaire Linda Wallis convinced herself — or at least her board — that it was extraterrestrial technology. She'd recruited Valley and Julian, a crew, and the *Prince of Cats* to go looking for 'live ones' in the Kuiper Belt. It was a crazy long shot, like Jefferson sending Lewis and Clark after mastodons. The media went crazy when Linda announced she was going herself. Valley hadn't believed the technology hype, preferring the biological explanation she'd defended in her thesis. But the promise of exotic tech, and Linda's force of personality, won the expedition ample funding.

And they did find 'live ones'. Whether they were biological or technological seemed irrelevant after that. They seemed to feed on icy bodies, floating between Kuiper Belt objects like motes of dust in a dark room.

Harmless, delicate, beautiful when the light caught them.

And now...

Something was crawling on her arm. It startled her out of her regrets. She grabbed at the spot that tickled, but found only cobweb. The feeling of the layers brushing against each other between her fingers and her forearm was firm and smooth, as if her skin were made of silk. It looked impossibly delicate — she could still see her brown skin through its iridescence — yet it was strong enough to keep her pressurized in the vacuum of space. The vibrations moved around her body, touching every part with varying strength before finally fading.

What is it doing? How am I alive?

It must be producing oxygen inside my respiratory system. She held her breath and counted. Thirty, sixty, a hundred and sixty... she didn't need to inhale. *OK that's not disconcerting at all.* She tried not to think about it, failed, started to panic again.

She was distracted by a light flickering across her shoulder. Then her arm.

At first she thought it was coming from a ship she couldn't see. She tried to look behind her, but without leverage it was impossible. As the glow steadily increased and moved across her body, she realized it was the cobweb making it, emitting light against every surface it touched. Just like the vibrations. *This is starting to feel like a calibration sequence.*

Wait. Was that it? Was it trying to communicate? Blindly trying every spectrum?

"Sound," she said. "I use sound! Talk to me!"

A vibration started in her throat, then moved out across her face and became a voice as it approached her ears. It was her own voice.

"Sound," it said. "I use sound! Talk to me!"

OK, space cobweb. This, I can do.

It might have been hours or millennia before they reached a planet. Valley's periods of unconsciousness were indeterminate, and each time she awoke, the stars were a mess. Constellations kept shifting, changing shape, and disappearing altogether. She didn't know enough astronomy to guess where the cobweb was taking her, but everything she knew about physics told her it was impossibly far. She assumed her periods of unconsciousness were long cryogenic sleeps — but how long? How much time had passed? Was anyone she knew still alive? Did it matter, if she had no way of ever going back? And where the hell was this thing taking her?

She killed her waking time by talking to the cobweb. It wasn't much of a conversationalist, but it learned to count eventually, and it could mimic anything she said. She named everything she could see out loud, which included body parts and stars and... that was it. She named the thing, officially, Cobweb.

And then, after countless sleeps, she finally woke to a horizon.

It was blue. The wrong blue. A gas giant orbiting a red sun. Clouds swirled and spun in lava lamp dances from pole to pole, turquoise and robin's egg and white. She watched it quietly, for hours, before naming it.

"Planet," she said.

"Planet," said Cobweb.

"Sorry I'm not more creative."

"Sorry I'm not more creative." She accepted its apology.

And just as a small, red-orange sphere rose over Planet's endless storms, she fell asleep again.

Dusty sand supported her when she woke, holding her hands and feet, arms and legs, neck and face against gravity. It felt strange to feel her weight again, and stranger to feel her face, nose and mouth buried in sand that didn't irritate her eyes or threaten to fill her lungs. Cobweb had set her face-down on this moon. How could it know she wasn't accustomed to slithering or rolling? It seemed to have simply dropped her in the position from which she was least likely to fall.

Inside the cobweb, she felt no difference between this atmosphere and empty space, and had no way of knowing if the air had oxygen, if it was cold, or what the wind felt like. She couldn't even taste the sand in her mouth. But at least it looked different.

She lay there for a moment, weakened by long-term weightlessness but also elated to be touching ground. Any ground. She couldn't feel the planet directly with her skin, but the cobweb was thin and she could feel the texture of the sand if she rubbed it between her fingers, the bumps of pebbles prodding her flesh.

When she did decide to stand, she realized she was far too weak. Everything had atrophied. And she was thin – emaciated, on the edge of starving. But not hungry. Cobweb made every molecule she needed, and nothing more.

"Come on, help me out. You brought us through Galaxy knows how much space but you can't help me stand up?"

"Come on, help me out..." Mindless repetition. She sighed.

The landscape reminded her of Mars. The odds were against this atmosphere being breathable by humans, but she had no way of knowing. She was in a space suit still — just a very thin, weirdly intelligent space suit that liked to kidnap exopaleontologists and happened to be equipped for interstellar travel.

Interstellar travel. The phrase echoed in her mind as her eyes followed the brownish-red horizon, the double-shadows of the rocks and dunes, and the blue giant in the sky whose reflected light made weak, blue double shadows. She was truly in another solar system.

Everyone... Julian, Linda, her crew, her parents... all gone with time. Julian's sobbing last words to her echoed across the plain. They were probably the last human words she would ever hear.

"Why did you bring me here?" she asked.

"Why did you bring me here?" Cobweb answered.

"Six days have passed," Cobweb told her the moment the red sun fell below the horizon. It was the first day it had told her on its own.

Valley smiled. It felt weird. She hadn't used her smile muscles in... how long?

The days were less objective than on Earth — she was on a moon, so there was the orbit of the moon around the blue gas giant she'd named Planet, and then there was the orbit of both bodies around the red sun. So some nights the gas giant was in the sky, and some nights it wasn't. And then there were eclipses, which were basically nights. All that considered, this moon's rotation felt like maybe half a day to Valley, and its orbit around Planet seemed only slightly longer. But she had no frame of reference except her own compromised biology.

"How many days since you kidnapped me?"

It echoed her, dumbly. She kept walking. It had learned how to support her weight and assist her movements, but nothing close to a concept as abstract as 'kidnap'. She didn't even know to explain 'take' without someone else from which to take something.

The sky was growing dark, but she wasn't tired and even if there was danger, there was no shelter. It really did remind her of Mars. A dead world. If Cobweb had creators, there was no evidence of them here.

She tripped over something, and fell hard into sand and rocks. "Dammit! Ow. You can protect me from the freezing vacuum of space but not from a stupid rock? Thanks a lot. Jerk."

It repeated everything back to her, including her childish outrage. She fumed silently while she picked herself up.

The rock she'd tripped over could just barely be made out in the light of the crescent blue giant.

Its edge was too straight. She dusted it off. Its right angles were worn smooth by wind, but it had definitely been rectangular once. Made of red sandstone.

There were more of them on either side of it and underneath. Identical.

She'd tripped over a wall.

Oh, hell. It thinks I'm an archaeologist. You and every cab driver and half my cousins.

"I'm a *paleontologist*, Cobweb. Exo-paleon-tologist."

And yet, looking over that worn right angle in the soft blue light, the magnitude of the discovery made her heart race. There could be fossils yet to be found.

Morning light revealed the outline of a buried city. She'd seen places like this as an undergrad, on the way to Mesozoic field sites in New Mexico. Unexcavated ruins, almost indistinguishable from the surrounding stone and sand until you start to see a pattern that nature doesn't make. Just take out all the sagebrush, and turn the sky a dusty orange, drop a blue gas giant in the sky and —

Holy shit, what is that? Something moved in the ruins and it wasn't masonry. A... blob... four or five times her size, lurched toward her.

It was wrapped in the same diaphanous material she was, grayish and shining gold where the sun hit it.

The blob had its own cobweb.

How long had it been here? How was it still alive? Where was it from? Was it dangerous? Was it intelligent?

It was shapeless, amorphous, moved like a galloping amoeba. It slowed as it came close, then stopped about four body lengths away from her. Was it afraid?

She waved. For a second she had a mental image of the naked couple on the Voyager plate and laughed — nervous, too loud — startling herself. The blob twitched.

It was flickering vivid purple patterns across its skin, under its cobweb.

"Blue," said Cobweb.

She shook her head. "Purple."

She looked down at her own body. Cobweb had perfectly matched the shade, on the outside. She was a vivid purple from head to toe.

She wanted to try something. "Red," she said. Her exterior turned red.

The blob lost its color. No red.

"Blue." She turned the precise color of the only blue around — the gas giant they orbited. The blob changed a dull purple. *Maybe it can only do purple,* she thought. *Maybe most of its light perception is in the ultraviolet range, and I can't even see ninety percent of what it's showing me.*

She tried something else. "One." Cobweb drew one line, a photographic replica in purple of the ones she'd drawn in the sand, across her chest. "Two. Three. Four." Cobweb kept up, adding lines as she counted.

The blob matched her at four lines. Then showed her five. "Five!" she said, and Cobweb matched it. The blob showed a sixth. "Six!" Cobweb translated. Blob went to seven.

Excitedly, she said, "Planet!" Cobweb displayed a vivid, photographic rendition of what she'd seen in space as they approached this world. A screengrab from the moment she named it. She couldn't see it all, but suddenly her hands were covered with stars, her legs and belly were the blue of the gas giant, and rising behind it, across her chest, was the unmistakable red-brown surface of the moon that all four of them now shared — human, blob, and the cobwebs covering each. *Where's your 'Sorry I'm not more creative,' now?*

Blob displayed a similar image, but in shades of purple, and from a different angle of approach.

She clapped her hands with delight. In response, Blob protruded two pseudopods and tapped their ends together.

I've made friends with an alien!

They walked the ruins together, stopping to dig at interesting spots. The city had been huge, and they spent days exploring. Valley wondered at first if Blob was from this planet, maybe some more habitable region, and if Blob's people had created the cobwebs — assuming the cobwebs had creators at all. But the way Blob poked and prodded at the stones the same way she did, curiously searching these ruins as if this place were just as strange to them as it was to Valley, convinced her they were in the same boat she was. Alone and far from home, wondering why they were here.

Another intelligence with its own cobweb in the mix gave Cobweb the chance to learn more abstract concepts, like "us," "here," and "there." Blob expressed themselves in flashing purple patterns and bulbous protrusions, no sound. She wasn't sure if they had eyes, but they seemed to see in every direction at once.

"Having someone else here," she rambled, knowing nothing would translate but needing to talk, "someone I can look at, walk side by side with — probably ride, but that seems rude — and talk to, sort of, it's incredible. It's the best. It's like a new best friend on the first day of kindergarten. And…" she said the next line over Cobweb's mindless repetition, "It's so fucking lonely, too." The words were lost in Cobweb's echoes. When they finally repeated back, she cringed.

When it had just been her, she could forget.

Now, Blob reminded her of everyone else she'd ever walked with. Everyone who was gone. She found herself telling Blob about thunderstorms and coffee and the *Prince of Cats*, and even though Cobweb couldn't translate basically any of it and had no idea what the *Prince of Cats* or even Earth was, Valley would trail off mid-sentence, choking on a name whose face she was already forgetting.

"My chatter must sound like birdsong to you," she said to Blob.

"Birdsong?" Cobweb asked.

Blob flashed inscrutable purple patterns.

Maybe they were rambling, too.

Thinking of Cobweb's calibration sequence, Valley realized she and Blob had a lot in common. Considering the vast range of strengths of different frequencies — what if Blob's bioluminescence had blinded her? What if her voice had deafened them? What if she'd towered over them and accidentally stepped on them, or vice versa? Shit, had she stepped on anyone already? What other beings were out there? How many worlds with ruins? What other languages did the cobwebs know?

Blob and Valley operated at comparable time scales — although sometimes Blob made lightning quick pattern changes, like flipping through the pages of a book.

She imagined Blob giving up in those ruins where she'd found them. Wandering for months — years — being kept alive by their cobweb. How long had they been there, staring at the ruined walls? If she hadn't found Blob, Valley could see herself sitting down one day and letting the sand bury her. Was that what Blob had been doing when she found them?

Day twenty-one (so Cobweb announced at sunrise) arrived with a question. Cobweb might finally be ready to answer it. "How long has this been here?" she asked, then had to spend the morning teaching Cobweb "wall" and "city" and exponents.

The short answer, which took four hours to get to, was that Cobweb didn't know.

"Come on, you work at a molecular level, you create oxygen and amino acids on the fly! You're telling me you can't do some simple radiometric dating?"

And as Cobweb repeated back every part it was confused about, which was all of it, she realized she would need to find something organic, or some material that had crystallized the same time the city was constructed. Glass might work. Masonry would only give the date the rocks were formed, and sandstone masonry would only give the date of the rock its sand was made of... and as she recited the fundamentals of her profession to herself, she had flashbacks to freshman geoscience... and for some reason that TA, Miranda, the one she'd had a crush on... and then she started to cry again.

Fuck this planet.

She yelled the thought as loud as she could, and kicked the sand.

Blob came up to her, protruded a lump near their base, and kicked the sand with it.

Valley was startled to hear her own laughter.

Excavating became their life. They conversed in purple shapes and sand drawings, while digging and digging and digging. Valley dug with her hands, Cobweb reinforcing them into trowels, and Blob moved vast amounts of sand with a shovel-shaped pseudopod.

Valley drew when they got tired. She taught Blob and Cobweb the alphabet, the positions of the stars she remembered from her own sky, silly symbols like hearts and smiley faces. She tried to teach Cobweb the different emotions, but it only seemed to understand them as chemical signals, which, when she thought about it, they were.

While Blob could replicate her sand drawings with perfect purple accuracy, Valley had no way of reproducing Blob's flashing patterns. She would have to name the patterns she noticed, tell Cobweb the name, and have Cobweb display it back to Blob. But she never noticed the same thing twice. Maybe the meaningful parts were outside her visible spectrum, faster than she could observe, or maybe her brain just wasn't built to recognize them. They would have to create a shared language in the media they had in common. Maybe their cobwebs could do the rest, eventually.

Cobweb now understood, at least sometimes, the difference between a statement and a question. That meant she could ask it things, and she discovered it was able to answer in pictures, displayed just in front of her eyes, in a kind of cave-painting-and-photograph head-up display. "Where is Blob?" returned a photographic rendition of Blob next to a rock or wherever they happened to be at that moment.

She drew her ship. The *Prince of Cats*. She made it as detailed as possible. Blob watched intently in their eyeless, faceless way, and displayed a perfect rendition of her drawing back to her, as creases and ridges in dust, sprawled life-size across their skin. She wondered if they even understood it as symbolic, or if they thought she was just playing in the dirt.

She looked intently at her masterpiece, and said, "*Prince of Cats.*"

"*Prince of Cats*," Cobweb agreed.

"Picture. Use picture." It obliged by showing her a perfect photograph of what she had just drawn, the same as Blob had done.

"Show me things like this that you and I have seen together." It displayed a series of rocks, patterns in the sand, features on hillsides. She kept shaking her head. Finally it showed a comet — a KBO? — that vaguely resembled the outline. Maybe it was going back in time.

There it was! "Yes! The *Prince of Cats*! Yes!" It held the image. She felt her eyes make tears at the sight of it, and she felt Cobweb absorb them before they could fall. The *Prince of Cats* was beautiful. It had been her home for two years. She'd done the most important work of her career inside that tin can.

Her throat knotted. The *Prince of Cats* was long gone. Its crew were dust.

Had they made it home? Had Istry finished his book? Had Omar ever asked Reed out? Had Julian ever forgiven himself for forgetting her tether? And Linda — that psycho. Had her investors been happy when the *Prince of Cats* returned down a crew member but up an observation? Had they ever figured out what the cobwebs were?

And her mom and dad. Had they coped...? *Oooh, Mom. I'm so sorry. Daddy...*

She stared into the sand. Were there more grains or regrets?

"How long has it been?" she asked, her voice choking up with chemical signals that only she knew were emotions.

"One thousand and twelve days," it answered.

How... Wait what?

She tried to guess how many Earth days that was. Maybe two years? How could that be possible? The *Prince of Cats* would barely be back near Saturn Station.

She needed to share this with Blob.

"Show the *Prince of Cats* to Blob," she told it. Blob displayed it back to her instantaneously, then surprised her by overlaying her sand drawing on top of it. It was all in shades of violet. She nodded and smiled. Blob protruded a bulbous appendage that nodded back at her.

"Tell Blob it's been one thousand and twelve days since we saw the *Prince of Cats.*"

Blob flashed violet patterns. They seemed contemplative.

"Cobweb, do you think Blob's species hugs?"

This of course was too abstract, even if Cobweb had any way of knowing what a hug was. Anyway, she didn't want to make Blob uncomfortable. So she drew a heart in the sand.

There must be something they were meant to find here, on this planet, some reason their cobwebs had brought them here.

The scientist in her kept digging, counting, drawing symbols in the sand.

One evening, when the blue giant had eclipsed its sun and the sky was filled with bright strange stars, Blob showed her their own ship. A purple cylinder floating in a purple star field appeared across their skin. The image panned around the ship, and then zoomed in on a star behind it. They'd composed a whole video.

"Is that your sun?" Their cobwebs translated what they could of the question from her sound into Blob's violet patterns, and Blob nodded a protrusion. She wasn't convinced they'd understood her question, though. Cobweb was still finding possessives a challenge.

"You're homesick." There was no translation. She tried something else. *"Prince of Cats."* Cobweb displayed her ship. Blob nodded.

Valley fell asleep staring up at the endless stars, filled with hopeless frustration she didn't know how to express.

It was a bright day. The sky was less dusty than usual and Planet was so crisp on the horizon she could see its clouds.

A good day for an abstract concept.

"Show Blob over by that wall," she said. Cobweb knew which wall she meant because she was looking at it; she didn't even need to gesture. Although to Cobweb, she supposed, a glance was just a gesture with a small wet body part.

It displayed an image of Blob near the wall. She got excited. Blob was not currently near the wall. They were right there in front of her.

Blob seemed excited too. They flashed purple, then, to her surprise and delight, lurched their way toward the wall, and stopped right where the image had shown them. She clapped her hands and nodded.

Blob nodded in response and clapped protrusions, then lurched back toward her.

An idea came to her as they approached, one of those ideas so obvious in retrospect you can't help but laugh to yourself out loud, and Valley did.

Cobweb had brought her here to meet Blob, not find the ruins. There was nothing in the ruins.

It had landed her near Blob and subtly directed her to Blob's location because their communication systems were so compatible. Or perhaps Blob was just the closest sentient lifeform of any kind. Either way — the goal of the cobwebs was to make introductions. That had to be it.

Perhaps Cobweb had not, after all, mistaken her for an exoarchaeologist. Of course they'd found nothing in the ruins. The ruins were incidental. They were meant to find each other.

Back at her side, Blob displayed an image of Valley standing by a large rock, about thirty feet away.

It was the first time she'd seen herself since she was on board the *Prince of Cats*. She was thrilled to see a human form, though it was purple, covered in the skintight cobweb, hairless and emaciated and effectively nude. She wondered briefly what non-living accessories Blob had started out with. She didn't know how to ask. Fur? Scales? A carapace? Clothes? Integument came in so many forms.

She stood up and walked over to the rock, just where Blob had shown her. Blob flashed purple, nodded and clapped. Valley did the same, except the purple part, and ran back over to Blob.

She grabbed a rock. "Take this over to the wall," she said. Cobweb didn't know what to make of "take this", but showed her the rock at the wall. "Show Blob and the rock at the wall." It obliged.

Blob protruded a limb toward her. She held out the rock in her hand. "Take," she said, as Blob picked up the rock from the palm of her hand.

"Take," Cobweb repeated.

Blob lurched back to the wall, and gently set the rock down at its base, where Cobweb had shown it.

She clapped and nodded.

Now for the real test. Cobweb had taken her light years against her will. Could it take her twenty feet on command? "Cobweb. Take Valley to the wall."

She felt her arms and legs move without her control. It was more terrifying than she thought it would be, but she tried to relax and let Cobweb move her. It was not unlike the way it assisted her movements normally, but totally giving up control was disconcerting and she kept tensing up involuntarily.

The movements were slow and jerky. Halfway there she felt a muscle cramp up, and her leg stiffened.

Cobweb stopped its motions and she fell over. Blob rushed to her side. They couldn't possibly understand that she was in pain, but they surely recognized motions that were unusual for her. Did they guess what she was trying to do?

Blob helped her up. She wondered again if their species hugged.

"How could I leave you alone here? We still have so much to learn about each other."

The next morning, when she was fully awake and sitting up in the sand, trying to remember what coffee tasted like, Blob approached her. They displayed their purple cylinder ship in its purple sky, extended a protrusion, and gently touched her arm. On the protrusion was an image of a heart, drawn in lavender sand.

Then Blob collapsed into a crumpled piece of laundry.

Their cobweb was empty.

"Blob?"

It ruffled slightly in the wind.

"No, no, no... Blob?? *Blob?!*" She crouched and reached toward the cobweb, then stopped short of grabbing it. It looked so fragile.

In the right environment, the empty, crumpled cobweb might, over time, be preserved between layers of sediment, and flattened into a fossil like the one she and Julian had found on that meteorite on Titan. The one she'd written her thesis on. The one that had started all this bullshit. The one that, eventually, had led her here, to Blob.

"Cobweb. Where is Blob?" She could hear the panic in her voice. Old terror crept back into her stomach, that fear of being eaten alive, the memory of the certainty of death when her helmet first caved in under the thousand microscopic mouths of a grey-gold film in space.

Cobweb displayed an arrow drawn in sand, a photographic replica of one she'd drawn when teaching it directions. It pointed up and to the left. Her eyes followed it until it hovered over a nondescript spot in the bright, dust-filled sky.

She remembered Blob's last message. The image of their ship.

"Cobweb, what happened to Blob?"

"Blob is not here."

"Damn it, Cobweb, I need a better answer! Is Blob hurt?"

"Blob is not hurt."

"Can I see Blob?"

"Can I see?" Cobweb didn't understand.

"Show me Blob." Cobweb showed Blob as they'd looked right in front of her the moment before they disappeared.

She sat in the sand and dropped her face into her hands.

Blob had left her alone, with only Cobweb and the silent ghosts of this nameless, galaxy-forsaken moon.

She woke in a dust storm. Cobweb protected her skin and eyes, but she couldn't see anything and didn't feel like doing anything even if she could have. She lay in the sand and let the dust cover her.

How many sentient beings were buried in cobwebs on ruined worlds?

She thought of the first time she'd met Blob, the way they moved toward her — excitedly, she now realized — across those ruins. The first time Blob touched two pseudopods together after she clapped her hands. She thought of Blob's excited purple flashing, and their shared moment of discovery when they taught their cobwebs 'take'.

Had Blob told their cobweb to take them away? To take them home? Could it be that simple? But how had they travelled? It had seemed instantaneous, and Blob had left their cobweb behind. Maybe Blob's species had some trick? Maybe they'd been rescued somehow?

Then another thought occurred to her. "Cobweb," she whispered, "take me to Blob's cobweb."

She blacked out.

When she woke, the dust storm still raged but the sand under her had shifted. She felt around. It wasn't anywhere in front of her.

She sat up. A crumpled, empty cobweb was just behind her, laying in the center of a human-shaped depression in the sand.

"Incredible," she whispered. That wasn't Blob's cobweb. It was hers. She was *in* Blob's cobweb now. It felt identical.

"How many cobwebs have I had?"

"Three thousand nine hundred and twenty nine."

It was her own voice, just like her cobweb had used. She'd realized the cobwebs must share information from the way they facilitated her and Blob's communication, but now it was obvious they were more intricately networked. They didn't just transmit information. They transmitted matter. That was why they didn't need propulsion. That was how they kept her and Blob alive on a planet that had only rocks and air.

There could be trillions of them. They could be in every solar system in the galaxy, undetected by civilizations like her own until adventurers like Julian and Linda and herself — and Blob — journeyed to their comet belts, where the cobwebs grazed and left trace fossils between accretion layers.

Blob had figured it all out, but hadn't known how to tell her. They could only show her by example.

And Cobweb. All the cobwebs. They couldn't just plant her on some inhabited world and expect the natives to treat her with respect — no, they had done this many times and knew how fucked up social species could be. They had to make introductions on worlds where two beings would be forced to become friends.

It had worked.

She thought of her ship mates. Linda's constant string of profanity, which had apparently rubbed off on Valley more than she'd realized, and the rest of the crew — Istry with his dark sexy shoulders and quiet hours writing. Omar and Reed's constant flirtation in the engine room. And Julian. Stupid, space-mad Julian who'd gotten her into this mess in the first place with a forgotten tether.

I am gonna kick your ass for this, Julian. ...After hugging you really, really hard.

Valley closed her eyes. It seemed like a good time for a deep breath, but she hadn't breathed in months, so she shrugged instead. *No way is this going to work.*

"Cobweb. Take me to the *Prince of Cats.*"

And the red world faded, and she fell asleep.

No spacesuit was needed. She floated outside the hull of the *Prince of Cats*, a layer thin as breath between her skin and the void. She was Valley, and she was Cobweb, and she was something else.

She'd come out here, to the Kuiper Belt, to find a fossil. Now she had a universe to share. A species of

Blobs to introduce them to. A story that actually involved space archaeology, for all those distant relatives who only half-remembered her profession.

Someone noticed her through the window of the starboard cupola. Linda. A coffee mug fell from her hand, brown liquid splashed against the pane. Her mouth formed the shape of a four letter word. She turned and shouted to someone out of view.

"Cobweb, are you picking up any radio signals?"

"Radio signals?"

Oh, there was still so much to teach this thing.

Someone else appeared in the window, next to Linda. It was Julian. He held up a piece of paper, letters hastily scrawled.

VALLEY?!!

"Valley," said Cobweb.

She nodded. "Would you write something back to him for me, Cobweb?" She spelled it out, and the letters appeared across her torso, replicas of ones she'd drawn in sand.

I'M OK!

NEED HUGS THO.

She wondered, as the airlock door inched open, if there was any hot coffee left. And then a terrifying thought occurred to her. What if she couldn't taste it?

"A Layer Thin As Breath" originally appeared in *Metaphorosis*, on 12 July 2019

About the author

Thea Boodhoo lives in San Francisco with an elderly tortoiseshell cat, a machine learning artist, twelve houseplants and an ever-increasing number of computers. She's been writing science fiction since third grade and recently started draft 4 of a novel about an AI-managed wilderness.

theaboodhoo.com, @tharkibo

The Shapeshifter Unraveled

S. Qiouyi Lu

Marie was thunder and lightning, a tornado tearing through the plains, weaponized rage consuming everything in her path. And I was a mouse clinging to a stalk of grass in the distance, watching her, trembling in the wake of her glory.

Envy swallowed me. I wanted to be her, a force of nature instead of this borrowed shape; I longed to be anything but what I was inside.

I became an oyster first. I drank salt water and plunged into the icy depths of the Pacific; I wanted to take the sand gnawing at me and turn it into something beautiful.

But all I did was eat grit and slice my insides. I bled and felt the emptiness within me, the hollow where a pearl should have been, where the perfection I saw in her should have echoed in me.

I tried again, this time becoming a peacock. I fanned my tail out until I became a cascade of emeralds and sapphires ringed with copper. Perhaps if I could preen enough, if I could boast enough, I could mimic her glory.

But I faded, my tail collapsing under its own weight. This was neither me nor her, the falseness tearing at me until I became a whirlwind of feathers.

Before I could settle back into my true skin, I became fire, raging as I consumed whole forests through the Sierra Nevada, leaving destruction in my wake. I wanted to be seen like her, to be feared, to strike awe like her, to have people witness my power, my rawness, the jagged edges of me whipping the air.

But after the embers faded, after I was left with only smoke-choked lungs and ashes, I remembered: I am nothing but this soft-fleshed thing, this utterly human thing, round and naked and vulnerable, this imperfect creature that is the only form I can claim as truly my own.

The next time I saw Marie was in San Francisco's Chinatown. I had given up pretending, resigned to my own odious body; I bumped into her as we were both entering a tea house.

I thought the tornado was her true form, but she was human just like me. I could still see the lightning in her eyes, hear the thunder coiled under her tongue; at the same time, I could see how tired she was, how small she'd become. She was lightning and thunder and glory, she was a tornado that could tear through one house and leave another unharmed, but she was destroying herself in the process.

We greeted each other warmly, and I offered to buy her a drink. We sat across from each other by a window, sunshine gleaming off our teacups. The silence between us was awkward at first, years of distance and casual acquaintanceship separating us, but then she spoke.

"I'm sorry for not being very chatty. Between my exhibition opening and the commissions I'm working on and the media attention—it's been a lot to deal with."

She set down her teacup, and I noticed then how delicate her wrists were, the jade bangle encircling her left wrist duller than my own. My father's words echoed in my mind: *A shiny bracelet is a mark of good health.*

"That's all right," I said. She smiled, the warmth of it making me blush—how genuine she was, always open; her emotions were what made her strong, what she poured into her work to give it life—and yet sometimes she poured too much, risking herself in the undoing.

"Have you been working on anything lately?" she asked.

I shrugged. "It's been difficult for me to paint recently. Just… a lot on my mind."

"I understand." She took another sip of tea. "For what it's worth, I've always admired your work. I know you think it's too simple, but there's a clarity to your lines, a cleanness to it that takes others years to master. I always feel like my work is too messy, too raw compared to yours."

"Thank you," I said. "It means a lot, coming from you."

She blew on her tea and took another sip. "I miss elementary school," she confessed as she looked out the window. "Do you remember how we used to run across the playground to that big tree and climb up into its branches?" She turned to look back at me. "I miss being friends with you."

"Me too," I said, and found myself surprised by the way my voice trembled, the way my heart clenched tight against my ribs. I'd spent so much time trying to be her that I'd forgotten what it was like to be *with* her, how I'd loved her and still did, how we weren't in competition but could work alongside each other.

"Will you be here for long?" I asked.

"I'm visiting family next week, but other than that, I'm here to stay."

Behind her lightning and thunder I saw someone more vulnerable, someone imperfect, and as she looked at me I felt something stirring within me too: my own force of nature, not destruction, but the shoots pushing out of the ashes in the wake of a fire, the soft hoofprints of deer cresting hills being reborn. I was not her and I would never be her, but I didn't need to be, either: I could just be myself, and trust that she saw the goodness in me, and that would be enough.

I reached across the table and placed my hand over hers. Calm washed over me and I felt settled in my own body, my true form, if only for a moment.

"It's not too late to be friends again," I said.

Outside, rain began to fall—a light *pitter-patter* that heralded no storm.

She smiled.

"I'd like that."

"The Shapeshifter Unraveled" originally appeared in *Daily Science Fiction*, on 22 October 2019

About the author

S. Qiouyi Lu writes, translates, and edits between two coasts of the Pacific. Their fiction and poetry have appeared in *Asimov's, F&SF*, and *Strange Horizons*, and their translations have appeared in *Clarkesworld*. They edit the flash fiction and poetry magazine *Arsenika*. You can find out more about S. at their website, s.qiouyi.lu.

The Guardian of Werifest Park

Carly Racklin

The train car reeked of cigarettes and rumbled like a storm. Loud enough to drown out the voice of every passenger crammed inside it, but still Inez's heartbeat rattled between her ears. It had started when she stuffed her backpack with clothes in the dark, and only boomed louder as she'd slipped out past her mother's wheezy, sleeping form on the couch, thirty-six or so hours earlier.

It had followed her through the cracked streets, then onto the bus, and all five trains after that. Or was it six, now? She hadn't slept a wink since the drumming started. She'd begun to think nothing would ever be quiet again.

The bruise on her cheek had faded enough now to be mistaken for a shadow on dusky skin, though it throbbed faintly in time with her pulse. No one had even spared her a passing glance when she boarded the train.

Inez had wedged herself into a far, windowless crevice of a seat, clutched her backpack hard against her chest, and waited for the dread to loosen its grip.

No luck yet. So onward it was.

Once her current train clanked into the station, she shuffled onto the platform and took a deep breath, only to taste even more bitterness in it. She reached into her pocket and drew out less than a dollar in change.

"Shit."

Strangers shoved past her and onto their trains. The longer she stood staring at those coins, the louder the dread rumbled in her skull. She needed to keep moving.

She drifted across the sprawl of washed-out tile, out of the paths of others who searched the flickering TV screens beseechingly. Everyone she passed was going in the opposite direction from her.

Inez stepped out into the stale summer air and walked. She walked until the afternoon bled into dusk and the day wasted away under the heels of her second-hand sneakers. She wove through gray streets flanked by gray buildings wearing more gray smoke like scarves. The hollow chill thickened in her gut with each step against the hard sidewalk, but she slogged on.

There had to be *something*. Something, not anything. No shelters—she wasn't a stray. A church could work. Hell, she'd take a bench at this point. Anything would do, so long as it wasn't that house.

Unlike her mother, Inez knew when to quit. When to give a place over to the vermin wasting it. The situation turned out to be comically simple, really. In the end, it all boiled down to a choice. Get out, or get wiped out.

Inez kept walking. Her stomach kept roaring, and her heart drummed on and on and on.

Then, the trees.

So many trees, all soft edges and swaying and green. An ocean of trees stretched to the sky and down the block and farther, farther than bleary eyes could measure. The first real trees she'd seen in days, wearing a collar of what was probably the sorriest excuse for a fence in the entire world. Inez jogged across the street and approached a large, slightly crooked sign.

TRESPASSERS WILL BE PROSECUTED. The words were printed in bold black type and hung against a background that at some point must have been white. PARK HOURS: 7AM-7PM.

The last dregs of sunset fell yellow and molten over the skin of her neck and the heavy padlock on the gate. Inez glanced over her shoulder to the city. Just looking at it made her itch to take a puff of her inhaler she knew she couldn't spare. No telling when she'd be able to refill her prescription again.

Despite the heat, Inez shivered, and a whisper from somewhere deep and dark in her chest asked, *What were you thinking?*

Behind her, the street was miraculously clear of cars. For one floating, dream-still moment, the only things breathing were her and those trees. Rustling, watching. Waiting to see what she would do.

She ignored the voice and climbed the fence.

Her feet hit the earth with a soft thud. She tore off her shoes and stuffed them into her backpack, sighing as grass eased the concrete's ache from her soles. Another sign accosted her a few strides in, this one so eroded it seemed ancient, hanging around the trunk of a tree like an amulet: a thirty-one point list of the park's prohibited activities. Vines and moss skirted its edges, entwined in the gaps of the chain that held it aloft.

No smoking, no hunting, no trapping, no littering, no fishing in the pond, no carving the trees, no, no, no. They would have saved a lot of paint if they'd just written KEEP YOUR DAMN HANDS TO YOURSELF. Inez wondered if there were security cameras in the park, but that would involve breaking about four of their own rules.

She ambled on until the fence disappeared from view. There weren't even any real footpaths, just vague stretches of faded grass, mostly concealed by the shells of parched leaves. *No digging. No vehicles.* Sounds of the city beyond waned with every step until they were barely memories. The dulcet crooning of unseen birds replaced the din of construction, of razing machinery. No sign of the skyscrapers, no sign of a single gray thing.

Huckleberries dotted the dark brush. Inez plucked them up in clusters as she walked, barely chewing, her relief turning even the most unripe clumps nectarous and intoxicating.

The path curved, and around the bend stood an enormous weeping willow. Under it: a bench. For the first time in weeks, maybe months, Inez laughed.

She sat down, shucked off her backpack, and took deep, even breaths. The air tasted sweeter than the berries.

But her clothes still smelled of her mother's cigarettes. So did the backpack, and the short dark coils of her hair. Now, though, in this park, the bitter smell seemed to have dissipated a little. Like the fresh air was washing her clean from the inside out.

Dusk elapsed in minutes; night draped the trees in obsidian. With the dark and stillness and her newly full stomach came syrupy fatigue. It colored everything— even the dingy bench was transformed into the softest and warmest bed she had known in years. For a long time, the only thing she did was breathe, letting herself sink further into the summer air, and it into her.

With every inhale, she imagined it purifying the black secondhand-smoke stains in her lungs, then sneaking into her veins and her brain, erasing every ugly thing that lived there, every memory molding in every dark corner and inside every wall.

Yes, she was alone in a city she didn't know the name of, broke and bedding down on a park bench. And there was a stubborn weight in her chest that she couldn't ignore, and bruises still clinging to her skin. But there were wild berries too, and trees tall enough to blot out the sky, and she didn't have to think of her mother ever again. For now, that would have to be enough.

The willow leaves rustled loudly above her, though the air was still. Inez couldn't bring herself to open her eyes again once they fell closed. So she just listened, and after a while, the rustling ceased.

She couldn't remember the last time she'd slept in air this clean, or the last time she'd lain in the night without listening to her mother slinking in the door with her latest fix. It was a different world entirely, a world made only of crisp, bright things. Balmy green things her mother's smoke could never spoil.

Inez slept like the dead, and dreamt of nothing at all. Until a sharp rattling cut through the gloom and jolted her awake into a dry early dawn.

For a moment the world reeled and her head spun, full of dizzy white flickers. She was stuck between spinning and floating, half numb still from the previous day's exhaustion. The rattling continued, and Inez jerked up from the bench when she recognized it as the sound of the metal fence.

The sun had just barely begun to light the park, like the first translucent strokes of an underpainting. What could it be, six in the morning? No way anyone was opening that gate right now.

But she hadn't needed to open the gate to get in.

The heavy crunch of footsteps sounded from nearby.

"Shit!" Inez hissed, and in a frantic blur, snatched up her backpack and dove for cover behind the thick trunk of the willow tree.

The footsteps lurched slowly nearer, down the same path she'd taken to the bench, and on. When they passed the tree, Inez held her breath, and leaned just slightly out into the open to regard her fellow trespasser.

Square shoulders, baggy jeans, dusty combat boots. The man plodding past couldn't have been much older than her, judging by his height and clothes. He stomped listlessly through the grass, clutching an aluminum can. Drunk.

He stopped walking a few feet past the bench. A lit cigarette teetered between the fingers of his free hand. He took a swig from the can, then a puff from the cigarette. The cloud of gray smoke he breathed into the air caused a queasy flutter in Inez's chest. Moments later, the scent hit her, and despite how hard she tried to fight it off, she couldn't breathe.

She hadn't smelled such strong cigarettes since her mother last lit one. That night could have been a lifetime ago, for how far away it felt. Ever since she was a little girl, any fresh whiff of that bitter smoke, and she was gasping, looking for fire, looking for ruin. She'd woken from nightmares of her mother turned to nothing but a heap of char on that ratty couch too many times to count.

When she was fourteen, the doctor had diagnosed her with asthma and recommended nicotine gum to her mother. And every night since for three whole years, Inez had slept with her window open and door shut.

Just when she thought she'd found the one place on earth where that smell couldn't follow her.

The man took another drag, his head lolling back with the inhale. Then he flicked the cigarette away, and it fell to the earth. The ashy end of it sputtered against the brittle foliage. Inez knew what came next, but when the orange flickers caught and burst outwards, she gasped as if she were the one burned.

The stranger whirled about. His glazed-over eyes met hers. Inez trembled and flinched, dropping back from her haunches into the dirt. Smoke drifted up from the ground in a thin curl.

A splitting thrum cut through the air. It sent a stabbing pain through the base of her skull, so loud it could have been coming from inside the bone. Like the whole forest had just trembled with her.

The willow tree above her shook violently again, without even a whisper of a breeze. The drunk man was not looking at her anymore, but up at the tree.

She followed his gaze to the branches. They weren't where she remembered them being.

The boughs bent to the ground, splayed apart wide like fingers. Inez took a breath that froze in her throat. Then the trunk of the willow tree uprooted from the earth.

It was much quieter than she would have ever guessed—to hear a tree tear itself out of the ground. For a moment, there was only a hum. Then a sharp crackle rippled through the stillness, and the trunk split in two. The halves met the ground, looking like the lean brown legs of a Titan. On either side of the tree, the remaining branches twisted into coils. Green vines dangled in a tight, roundish cluster at the willow's crest: a faceless head glistening with dew.

Inez had barely heaved in a new breath when the tree-thing angled its colossal semblance of a body toward the drunk man. At his feet, the cigarette still sputtered, glowing like a shrunken sun but giving no life. It would drain the green from anything it touched.

A yowl, like the groaning of a twig right before it snaps, sounded from the bundle of leaves atop the tree. It stuck in Inez's ears, in her teeth, in her ribs. It clashed with the piercing blare that the lit cigarette had conjured and for all she knew they were the same thing. Maybe that was what everything sounded like when you were going to die.

Inez's body moved separate from her mind. She crawled toward the cigarette on her hands and knees, and the willow moved too, overtaking her in one heaving stride. The drunk man had already started to run.

The whole world was rattling and that cigarette was still burning in the grass, like her mother, poisoning everything, and she couldn't breathe. She had to make it stop. In her peripheral vision the tree creature continued to move, its gnarled limbs cleaving through the air.

Inez mirrored it, throwing out her arm and smothering the cigarette against her hand. Ahead of her the creature halted, one of its branches seizing up mid-swing. The man disappeared into the brush and out of sight. When the metal fence jangled sharply in the distance not long after, the creature lowered its arm.

Inez's vision blurred. Panic pounded in her skull, almost loud enough to drown out the giant's gait as it turned back and thumped toward her.

Her chest burned with emptiness. She fumbled in her pocket for her inhaler. Blackness choked every thought in her head except the ones steering her hands.

Nothing left to exhale. *Click. Hiss.* Breathe in—hold—breathe out.

It took three puffs for the vise around her lungs to loosen. The world came slowly back into focus with every heave, centering on an ugly red burn glaring up from the center of her palm.

A tall shadow crashed over her. Inez looked up, breath thin again.

The creature had no eyes to meet but its stare still pierced. It stood rigid, a monument of bristled greenery. Tears welled up in Inez's eyes. Either from fear or pain, she wasn't sure. It didn't really matter, because she was going to die any second now. The creature craned its verdant body downward as if in confirmation.

Inez snapped her head down, closed her eyes, and waited to be crushed. Waited like she had those nights ago, back pressed to her bedroom door as it rattled with the force of her mother's fists, the air bloated with cigarette smoke and a voice screaming out for her blood.

She'd thought her mother was still sleeping off her latest bender when she flushed the pills. But her hands just wouldn't stop shaking, and everything had clattered to the floor, and she'd only gotten a few handfuls down the pipes when fingers had twisted into her hair and wrenched her back. A hand had crashed against her cheekbone, knocking her into the wall. Her ears rang and her mother had slipped on the tile, so Inez ran. She'd locked herself in her room and wept until long after her mother had given up on threatening to strangle her.

She'd made her decision before the latch even clicked. The next time she ran would be the last.

Curled in on herself in the dirt, Inez let the tears fall. Choked whimpers leaked through her teeth, clenched tight against the smoke. It could have been her mother there, all smoldering ash. Geared to snuff her out like an ember into a cracked tray.

Inez waited to die.

And waited. And waited.

Something soft brushed down her cheek. She gasped and the aroma of damp foliage flooded her mouth.

Rustling surrounded her. A faint creaking joined it, lurking just beneath the steady hum of leaves. Alike in timbre to what had sounded in the chaos, but with none of the venom—the same voice, a different tone. She blinked the tears out of her eyes. The green mop of vines hung just a few inches from her face, the rest of the creature bent in an awkward, jointless attempt at kneeling.

It didn't crush her. Instead, it raised one of the branches from its side and took her gingerly by the wrist of her burned hand. The long sprigs of leaves drew open her fist. This time, the noise that rose from the creature's unseen mouth was nearly a chirp, the pitch of it leaping, like a question. Shrill with curiosity, maybe even concern.

Before she could dwell on how pathetic that thought was, the giant punctuated its remark with a tilt of its massive leafy head, and sparks stirred in Inez's skull.

It was *talking* to her.

She searched for any hint of eyes behind those vines. "I ... um, I don't understand," she muttered, unsteady with the new weight of this wonder. But it was true: she was still alive, and a beast dressed in forestry had really just materialized because someone burned the grass.

She looked to the gray smudge between the two of them, where the extinguished cigarette lay, then at her palm, cradled by the willow's wispy fingers. "It burned you too."

The vines around her hand drew upwards a fraction, and a thin stream of clear water trickled out from a fissure in the branch and washed over her ash-dotted palm. She flinched and hissed at the sting.

The willow made a cooing noise that sounded an awful lot like the calming hums other people's mothers made to their fussy children. Had it learned that from observation? Or did nature have its own language of tenderness?

"Thank you," Inez said, brushing her fingers over the bark.

Again that rustling echoed around them, and the giant let her go. It rose with a chorus of creaks and trod heavily back toward the patch of ragged earth behind the bench.

Sunlight broke through the canopy and gilded the grass so fiercely Inez had to squint. Soundlessly, the earth began to knit itself back together once the rooted feet of the willow settled into the hollow they'd created. Time seemed to move in reverse as its limbs unwound and stretched to their original shape. By the time she blinked the brightness away, the bench and willow tree stood perfectly undisturbed, the burn in her palm the only indicator that any of it had ever happened.

Inez pushed herself up on two wobbly legs and teetered over to the tree, a small grin fighting its way across her face. She hitched her toppled backpack onto her shoulder; it weighed practically nothing now. One errant breeze and she might just float away like a petal, sheer and light enough to never touch the ground again.

That didn't sound so bad.

When she was just a little girl, 'never' had been the scariest word in the world. A cage that would suffocate her if she got too close. But now, 'never' was more secure than anywhere. Not a cage, but armor. She could lie down inside it and it would keep her safe.

Never was a survivor's word.

She'd whispered it in the din of every train, to the dread each time it returned and choked the breath from her chest—*never, never, never.* She was never going back.

And the dread was quieter now, like she'd finally gone far enough.

Inez rubbed her fingertips gratefully over the knobs and valleys in the willow's bark.

Someone would be opening that gate soon. If she were careful, she could get out before anyone knew she'd entered at all. She would be anonymous again.

Anonymous, but not free. Not free of the dread, or the smoke, or the exhaustion of searching for hope in a colorless city.

At least this place had rules. Rules meant care, and she'd seen precious little of that for a long, long time.

Inez pressed her ear to the willow. She didn't know what she expected to hear, but when it was silent, she couldn't stop her heart from sinking.

"Hello?" she mumbled, and rapped against the wood lightly with her knuckles. "Are you still there? I, um, didn't realize this park was already occupied." Her chuckle came out crumpled like the leaves dappling the undergrowth. No reaction. Maybe it was sleeping. Maybe it just wanted her to shut up and leave it alone. Or maybe it didn't care about her at all, so long as she didn't break any of the rules.

Leaving it be seemed like the safest bet. She didn't want to test the limits of its hospitality, not after what she'd just witnessed.

Feeling childish and yet vaguely like she was being watched, Inez started off in a new direction, away from the pseudo-footpath she'd first followed and into the brush. The noisy layers of expired leaves crackled like tinder with each stride.

By late morning, the air swelled with heat. She downed one of the water bottles she'd had the good sense to buy during her train-hopping, and had half-stuffed the empty plastic shell into her backpack when the sound of real running water hit her, muffled a little by distance. She followed it until her bare feet pushed through a hedge and slipped into blessedly cool mud.

A thin stream wound through the clearing. On its bank, hundreds of yellow flowers gleamed from spray cast off the rocks. Inez propped her backpack up against a tree, sat down on the edge of the brook and dipped her legs into the cool, glossy water. She splashed a handful over her face and scrubbed the scum of the last few days away.

Sighing, she shut her eyes and lay back against the bed of flowers. Her fingers carded through their velvety leaves, tight and tangled like her own curls. Her head went woozy with the blossoms' sweet scent.

She listened for any sounds of the city, knowing it lurked on all sides of the park. Still nothing. If the skyscrapers were teeth, then this forest sat in the middle of a wide-open jaw, surrounded on all sides but never devoured.

Something was different here—she'd noticed it before, but not realized how deep the sensation ran. It wasn't just the air, or the trees, or the ground. It was everything.

Her thoughts drifted again to that list of rules. It hung in her mind in the same looming way it hung on its tree, fixed in place even by the foliage. Different from everything else, but not unwelcome.

Inez opened her eyes, and swallowed a yelp. A figure hovered over her, though that was all she could really call it. Its vaguely human-shaped body was comprised entirely of clustered leaves and budded flowers. It seemed to watch her, though the closest thing to eyes it possessed were two blossoms just slightly larger than the rest, fixed at the middle of its lumpy crown.

She sat up and turned around to face the thing. Its maybe-head followed her. It looked like some kind of artsy hedge trimming from a magazine. Like someone had tried to haphazardly sculpt a person out of foliage, someone who didn't know for sure, or didn't care to know, exactly what people looked like.

"Oh, there are more of you," Inez blurted, heart still racing. Rustling filled her head. She held up her burnt hand and gave a short wave.

The leaves on the creature shook slightly, back and forth.

Inez worked her bottom lip between her teeth. "No? You're . . . just one?" She gestured over her shoulder back toward the general direction of the willow.

Another hum, then all the flower buds on the creature's body bloomed into striking tiny suns. The blossoms skirting the stream repeated the display, petals flaring out in a long wave. Warmth so far from the summer's unflinching aridity saturated the air; she breathed in and felt it in her chest, searching for soil to take root in.

Inez smiled, and caressed the leaves below her again. The little red dot glared up from her palm beneath the vegetation, a reminder of the damage already done, how they'd both been burned. A handful of soft gestures wouldn't erase that.

But it was better than nothing. Or so she hoped.

Inez watched the creature watching her, and wondered if it felt her touch like it had felt the cigarette. Maybe it felt everything the forest did, every inch of every acre. Like veins, connecting each life to the next, tying blade of grass to sprawling tree to sunning flower, each to each to each. A system, and its heart. What a thing to share a wound with.

"Those rules back there are yours, aren't they? They were written for you," she said.

Thirty-one rules was nothing compared to all the ways a thing could be hurt. All the ways a life could be snuffed out. No death too small to grieve. Like it ignored no offense, no wrong. Carrying a memory as old as earth.

Inez saw it all again: the cigarette, and the man, and the creature's arm raised knifelike in the air. A threat, and a response. She'd only seen it respond like that once, but judging by that sign, she guessed it had happened before, and often, who knew how long ago. How many small wars had the creature waged before someone had taken pity on it and written the restrictions that hung over the place?

Too many, of course. It was always too many.

The sun retreated and plunged the bank into shadow. She looked up, but found her vision swimming. The creature was closer now, an unreadable blur of gold and green. Inez shuddered under its unyielding stare. Her smile grew heavy on her face, and fell away without a sound.

She peeled her limbs away from the flowerbed and stood. Papery yellow petals came away with her, stuck with sweat to her skin. The moments of her life from before then unspooled behind her eyes, faded by time but still clinging like old stains to the fabric of her memory. She didn't want them.

Her heart pounded. "Do you want me to leave?" Inez asked in a small voice.

The creature gave no response. The warmth in her chest turned sour.

"Do you?" she said, louder now, though a shameful crack in her voice split the word. Dread wormed a cold trail through her. She didn't need an answer to know it was true, but the miserable reality of it hollowed out her chest. She swallowed down a sob.

The creature's form shrank back at the accusation, all of its flowers returned to buds.

It wouldn't have been the first thing to want her gone. Wouldn't have been the first place better off without her.

Inez knew pity when she saw it. It looked just like disdain, but with a prettier face.

She stumbled back a step, then another, until the hedge she'd first emerged from brushed her ankles.

She really hadn't learned anything, had she?

"I'm sorry," she mumbled. Her feet scrabbled for purchase on uneven ground. "I just wanted—I just—"

Inez turned and ran. The tears finally fell as she lurched through the bushes, over brittle grass and twigs that jabbed like needles. Each one another twist of the knife, a reminder of what she had known before ever climbing that fence but had refused to admit.

She didn't belong here.

But it was worse than that, and she knew it. She didn't belong anywhere.

A root smacked her ankle, and Inez tumbled into the dirt with a weak yelp of pain. Every heaving of her breath scorched like swallowing a red-hot sword. She pushed herself up on limp arms. Stinging outside and in, she clambered backwards until she hit a tree's gnarled trunk, decked in winding dark leaves. Then she hugged her knees to her chest and wept into her hands.

She wished the earth would just swallow her up. If she could just bury all her deluded fantasies and dissolve into the soil, maybe something good and useful would finally grow out of her, something that deserved to be there in that fence, a part of that system.

Loved. Or worth loving, anyway.

And that was just it.

The nameless weight beneath Inez's ribs swelled and flooded her chest with a gloom blacker than her mother's lungs.

She couldn't breathe, again. She fished out her inhaler from her pocket and took a puff, barely able hold it steady. The last time she'd triggered an attack from crying had been the night she flushed the drugs. She could almost smell the smoke again. Could still feel the grain of her bedroom door grate against her shuddering back.

Her breath returned in gasps, a thousand aches with it.

Just barely, on the edge of the forest's din, Inez heard rustling. The foliage beneath her shook.

A whorl of vines crept away from trunk and curled around her, covered in enormous scarlet roses. The mass encircled her in moments, overflowing with the balmy scent of petals. She gasped, and a rose-dappled vine reached out and swept over her bruised cheek, wiping away the last tear still inching down through the grime.

Something had grabbed hold of her lungs again, and her heart too, and held them with such puzzling fortitude and tenderness that Inez thought she would weep again.

The mass of vines and roses embraced her. Softly and resolutely. Tenderly and fiercely. The way her mother used to, before everything went wrong. She'd forgotten what it felt like.

She exhaled and sank into the creature's arms. Links of thornless blooming vine cradled her, stroking her hair in the same smooth motions her hands had used in the patch of flowers back by the stream.

"Why are you doing this?" she whispered. "I'm just the same as them."

A low hum reverberated from deep in the petals, but Inez couldn't decipher its meaning. The creature only held her tighter when she made no reply.

Inez breathed until the pain in her throat subsided to a faint prickling numbness. She wanted to lie down until she remembered nothing of her mother or the gray-stained house she'd run from. But the memories clung to her bones like weeds. She wondered if she would ever be able to uproot them without also uprooting herself. If she would ever be as green and blooming and free as the things that held her inside the fence.

Hesitantly, Inez reached into the leaves and returned the embrace.

The creature's silken-edged form stiffened, then recoiled. The climbing roses and vines receded, slumping limp against the trunk.

By the time she'd gasped and called out brokenly after it, the creature was already gone. Inez stood. Confusion struck her first, then cold terror. Something was wrong. Goosebumps mottled her bare arms and legs. She stared hollowly into the horizon for a long time.

When a breeze blew, she tasted smoke on it.

Not the bitter tobacco, lung-rotting stuff. Worse. The kind that swallowed houses and skin. The kind that cooked.

Inez went rigid. All the green around her swayed as one vast wall, revealing almost nothing. No more than a few slivers of sky to search, and no sign of the stench's source.

"Move, just *move*," she spat at her quaking knees. "Where are you?" she cried up at the trees.

No answer.

Then, voices. Men's voices, the words turned garbled and staticky by distance. The murmurs became yelling, and by the time Inez had turned in their direction, three men careened out of the trunks' thick barricade.

They nearly barreled into her, but the one leading the charge skidded to a stop just inches in front of Inez. His scuffed combat boots kicked up a small cloud of dirt.

A flock of birds scattered noisily from the treetops.

"Holy shit," he whispered. Inez flinched at the rancid booze on his breath. "It's you."

Two others crowded at his back. They could have been triplets, for their shared tawny hair and pasty white faces. A lopsided tattoo of a tiger stared directly at her from one's bare shoulder.

Inez blinked, unable to call any words to her tongue.

"I told you someone else was there," Combat Boots said over his shoulder with a laugh. He stepped toward her, and she stumbled back in turn. Her pulse boomed in her ears.

"Who cares, dude? Let's get the hell out of here," interjected one of the others, grasping his friend by the shoulder and giving it a good shake. Shaggy hair obscured most of his face, except for a lip ring that glinted in the sun.

Combat Boots laughed louder. His right hand clutched an open lighter, the flame thrashing.

All the warmth drained out of Inez.

"I was right. All along—about everything, I was right. What do you think of that, assholes?" he howled, turning on his heels. Inez barely ducked out of the lighter's arc.

Tiger Tattoo stepped aside. "You're out of your damn mind!" he scoffed. "I'm not about to die here."

The smell of the smoke was stronger now. Past the undulating trees, Inez thought she glimpsed a smudge of gray. "What did you do?" she muttered, slack-jawed.

She took another step back, but Combat Boots swung around and seized her wrist. She yelped; his bony fingers held deceptively strong.

"Let go of me." She tugged hard, but he clamped down harder. "*Ow*—stop! Let *go*!"

A tremor traveled up her legs from the ground.

Lip Ring and Tiger Tattoo glanced at each other, then broke out running, following their original course into the treeline.

Another tremor, then another. Softly, in the back of her skull, a familiar hum sounded.

"You know I'm right. You were right there with me," Combat Boots ranted, pressing his pale, pocked face in close.

Inez had readied a leg to kick him where it would hurt, when thundering footsteps broke in. The air smelled like death.

The treeline shattered open.

Inez barely recognized the willow. Swirling fire engulfed its extremities, each wispy vine a wick. Dark billows rose thickly from its upper half. It looked hasty, incomplete, the trunk barely divided enough for movement. It limped forward, and each ungainly step filled the air with a cacophony of dreadful cracks. Behind it, a trail of red and black cut into the park as far as Inez could see.

The air was kindling.

She wanted to scream, but her lips formed useless shapes around nothing and made no sound. Combat Boots' grin melted away. He released her arm and ran.

The willow screeched, heaving after him. One leg splintered apart as soon as it met earth, and the whole creature teetered, then came crumpling thunderously down. Breathless, she couldn't call out for it.

Embers flew, swallowing the brittle foliage in a flood of char. The willow craned the blackened remains of its head down and made a high, broken sound, then collapsed in a tide of cinders.

Tears and smoke burned Inez's eyes. She whipped around and around, but couldn't find the trees, or the sky, or the creature. Ash coated her tongue and crept down her throat no matter how she coughed. She fell to her knees and wheezed helplessly.

Everything was falling apart again.

Nowhere to run. The air was red, her sweat was red, her thoughts were red.

There was a choice, a choice. What was it?

Inez reached for her inhaler.

Get out—

But it was gone.

—or get wiped out.

Darkness descended. It swallowed her whole and washed away the scorched clearing. A rough and solid slab slipped under her legs and hoisted her up, and up, and up from the ground. She scrabbled for balance, gasping weakly. Her fingertips scraped bark.

Cracks of light revealed the mass shielding her: a thick canopy of leaves.

Inez reached out to touch them, and her inhaler fell into her palm with a muted thump. She took two doses. On her first good breath she tasted foliage, then hacked out black dust.

The tree lurched into motion. The branch beneath her shifted and nestled her against the upper part of the trunk. She heard the distant crackle of fire, and vaguely smelled the smoke. More than anything she felt the rocking of the tree, of the giant as it walked, cradling her against its bulk.

Lost for words, she took deep, grateful breaths of the mossy bark. Tears streamed through the dust on her face, over her cracked lips, and onto the tree.

She was alive.

Seconds or minutes or hours passed before the creature creaked to a halt, and Inez's forehead lightly smacked its rough flesh. The limb that held her curled up and drew her away from the trunk.

Air crashed over her. The shield of leaves unraveled and bared her to the sunlight. She blinked, and saw the chugging smoke leaking from the center of the park, how glowing fire split the trees with crimson light. For a moment she soared, weightless, against the bleeding sky. Then the branch that bore her stretched and tilted. She slipped from bark to concrete.

Sidewalk chilled her feet. A shape heaved through the air and smacked the pavement: her backpack.

The creature pulled away, back toward the burning forest.

Inez howled with every last shard of herself, "*No!*" She shot forward, fingers grasping the rusted fence.

The creature's limbs groaned as it withdrew, unheeding. Fear thundered in her skull. She hauled herself halfway up the fence in an instant, until the tree turned back to her in a creaking blur. Bark met her shoulders, leaves pried her fingers open. Together they pushed her, struggling, back down to the pavement.

Sirens resounded from the verging streets.

"Don't go back in there." she rasped, fresh tears stinging in her eyes.

This couldn't be happening. It couldn't save her just to disappear again. She was so tired of being left, of being alone.

"It's too late. You'll burn."

The creature replied something just as broken. Still, it pushed her to the sidewalk.

"Don't, please. Stay with me," she cried, clutching the branch and tugging it closer. Leaves caressed her face.

The giant murmured quietly and pressed itself into her hands for just a moment, then pulled away. Behind the fence, the creature turned and stomped back into the forest as fire engines pulled up on the street, and Inez wept, drowned out by the sirens.

When figures began to pour from the trucks, she scrambled across the street and deposited herself on a bench beside a dried-up fountain. Flocks of chattering onlookers crowded at the fence as the minutes drew on and smoke stole the color from the sky. None spoke to her, and she didn't speak to them.

Once she turned her back to the park, and the fire, and all the clamor of the scene, she didn't look back. She wouldn't.

It was what she'd done when she left her mother. She made her choice and knew not to turn around, but not because she'd go back if she did. She couldn't look back and move forward at the same time. She had to choose. So she chose running. She chose a future, just like she'd done before.

Dread and shame roiled together in her chest. She'd had no right to beg a guardian to abandon its duty, its home, for her. She was nobody.

She'd been so naïve, thinking that running away was the same as escaping. The same as healing. But distance had nothing to do with it. There was no escaping the past, just learning to carry it.

Her mother, that house, they were just memories. Soon the park would be too. There were so many hollow places in her now; she had more than enough room to keep them safe. She could carry them forever.

Inez sat quietly for a long time. Then she put on her shoes and walked to the train station.

Inside, the building was even colder than before, with polished floors that squeaked with every footfall. She passed at least ten TVs, their screens all flashing red, alternating headlines reading, FIRE IN OLD LANDMARK WERIFEST PARK. AUTHORITIES RESPONDING TO REPORTS OF UNIDENTIFIED FIGURE SEEN WITHIN.

Groups huddled beneath the television sets, their eyes squinted, gesturing emphatically at the footage of the fire, but Inez was too far away to see what captivated them. They paid no mind to her or her ash-caked clothes.

She washed herself clean in a bleached white bathroom. The soap smelled harsh and fruity, and it erased the must of scorched earth from her skin. When at last she scrubbed at the tracks her tears had left in the dirt on her face, the door squealed across the tile, and a woman walked in.

Contorted over the sink, Inez froze, and the stranger did too. She was blonde, with ivory skin, and wore a red pantsuit. Her eyes examined Inez with scalpel sharpness for only a second, then softened to glimmering amber.

Droplets of lukewarm water ran down Inez's chin and puddled on the floor. The woman's hands flexed around the handle of her purse. In a saccharine voice that could only belong to a teacher of small children, she asked, "Are you all right, dear?"

"Yeah," Inez said.

"Are you sure?"

She wiped her chin. "Yeah."

The woman's lipstick was the color of freshly bloomed roses. "Do you . . . need anything? Is there anything I can do for you?"

"Yeah."

The woman bought her a ticket for the train. When asked where she wanted to go, all Inez could think to say was, "Somewhere green, with no fences." No more skyscrapers, no more smoke, and no more living things in cages. She was sick of suffocating.

They stood together on the platform afterward, and Inez thanked her, clutching her ticket. The woman just smiled, nodded, and pressed her hand on Inez's shoulder briefly. She watched the slight jerk of the woman's eyes as they flickered between her face and the news still playing on the TV behind her.

She expected some kind of warning. A *"be careful out there"* or, *"take care of yourself."* But all she said was, "The world is a very big place, you know. It's easy to get lost in."

But it's not, Inez wanted to say. *It's not. It's very small. And everything burns just the same everywhere. Burns again, and again, and again. The only thing that changes is who gets blamed.*

No words came. The woman smiled blankly, then turned and left, and so did Inez.

Practically deserted, the train started off with a metallic screech the moment Inez sat down. She let her backpack slide off her shoulders. A tunnel swallowed the car in darkness, and sleep stole her away before the light returned.

When she woke, the train was still moving, but the city was long gone. The woman had slipped her some extra cash before leaving, which she'd spent on a ridiculously expensive sandwich at the nearest food cart to her track. She scarfed the whole thing down in huge, graceless bites. Her stomach soured and ached after that, so she pulled her knees to her chest and stared out the long, scuffed window at the landscape whistling by.

The train passed sun-bleached hills dotted with sparse, squat houses, though for the most part, the land was sprawling and desolate. The weights in her chest shifted and settled and scratched at her like a bundle of needles. The train car was gray and the upholstery smelled just faintly of cigarettes.

Inez put her head into her hands. A soft rustling sound stirred between her ears.

She jerked up, and found bright flickers dancing in her peripheral vision. She turned to the window.

A swarm of golden petals floated astride the train, undulating like a murmuration. Inez gasped, then keened, and pressed her burnt palm to the glass.

A cluster of petals pressed back, vaguely in the shape of a hand.

"The Guardian of Werifest Park" originally appeared in *Metaphorosis*, on 27 September 2019

About the author

Carly Racklin is a fantasy and horror writer from New Jersey. Her fiction has appeared in *Metaphorosis Magazine, The NoSleep Podcast, Luna Station Quarterly,* and more. She is especially passionate about trees and birds.

carlyracklin.com, @willowylungs

Earth Epitaph

R. Jean Mathieu

Five thousand years before the end of the Earth, the star called WR-104 went supernova. Over the intervening centuries, its deadly gamma-ray burst hurtled across silent planets and empty space on a death-errand to that distant world. And, in the intervening five thousand years, Earth learned to listen, and learned to see, and learned to contemplate its coming demise.

Mount Pleasant Radio Observatory was far from the chaos of downtown Hobart, and the roads were blocked, but it was only a matter of time.

Campbell shut the door behind her and, for all the good it would do, turned the latch.

"How're things here?"

Robinson glanced at the readout. "Arecibo went offline, and Socorro...and Dominion, in BC."

She turned back to the black Canadian. Campbell's jaw was set. "I'm sorry, luv. Any luck out there?"

Campbell hadn't found anything but a few old teabags. They had no mugs, so she made Lipton's in little Dixie cups, and joined Robinson at the monitors.

"Arecibo..." Campbell breathed. "They fired off the message, right? To the M13 cluster? Big deal in my history books, but..."

"Yes-s-s, I remember." Robinson made a face. "I was just a little girl. I wondered how aliens were supposed to understand what we were saying when I couldn't. And with just a weak radio pulse."

"Not like anyone'd mastered stellar resonance by then." Campbell replied.

"Thanks much for that, luv." Robinson nodded. Her face turned sour. "It wouldn't be *hard*, now we understand the principles. Could turn the sun into a giant telsat, if we wanted. Light her up so bright you could see it from WR-104. Leave a bloody *message*!"

Both women settled into their teacups, thoughts stuck on the gamma-ray burst.

Campbell spoke.

But why stop there? Could trap the signal in the sun's magnetosphere, let it broadcast once each rotation until the sun goes nova."

Robinson glared at her.

"Because Fermi, luv." She turned away, toward the monitors. "Active SETI's fine if you still believe in little green men. But the Great Silence..."

"Don't we *have* the solution to Fermi's Paradox?"

"Sure. Which of the dozen?" Robinson still looked away.

"Annis' Phase Transition hypothesis. It's only in the last billion years that gamma-ray bursts have been infrequent enough to allow advanced civilization..."

Robinson grunted.

"*Charlotte!* GRBs're getting less frequent as time goes on. It's Silent out there now, but it won't be for long. We're just...early to the party."

Robinson didn't speak, only sipped her tea and turned over Campbell's words. When she turned around, something in her eyes was more maternal than scholarly.

"Fair enough, MacKenzie, fair enough."

Campbell nodded. Robinson finished her tea, and refreshed it. She sat back, listening to the creak among the buzzing and whining.

"Well," she started, "if there're proto-civilizations out there, they might...listen. First thirteen primes, to get their attention, then code a message through polarization modulation...at the very least, they'll know we were *here.*"

Campbell's smile was thin, tired, and warm, like Campbell herself.

"*Hóson zêis phaínou...*" She sang. "Think I've got just the message in mind."

Robinson's wheels were already turning.

"...Have to wait for sunrise, at least. We'll hit Sol ourselves. No relays. We don't know if anybody's even alive to relay *to.* And for your heliotrans to work, timing's going to have to be perfect."

"Yeah, and we'll need to modify the array some, hook it up to the generator direct for sure..." Campbell bit her lip, a girlish gesture on her seamed face. "One of us is going to have to go out there."

As one, they turned to the window. Out there, Hobart burned, framing the antenna dish array in glowing shadow.

"I'll go." Campbell said, and tried to smile. "Age before beauty."

Robinson opened her mouth, but Campbell waved it off. "It makes sense. Your specialty was signal analysis, I worked with transmitters. You stay here and code the message, I can make the adjustments. And we'll..."

Both women looked into their Dixie cups, into the distant fires.

"...well. We were *here.*"

They finally slept, on empty bellies, around midnight. When Robinson's aching bones let her rise, Campbell was already packed – two water bottles, a radio, and a few hand tools in an old museum tote. She let herself out quietly.

Robinson busied herself with calculations...how much power and at what time and a thousand other factors... and kept the two-way radio humming at her left elbow. Campbell gave regular updates.

"At the array!"

"What was that? Ah. Only a squirrel."

"Power's on!"

"Up in the rafters. I can see Hobart from here..."

Her voice hurt, now. Probably thinking of her grandson in Montreal. Robinson acknowledged, kept working.

"Okay," Robinson said, peering at her monitor, "what message are we coding? Can't be too long...our moment of coronal repeat's in six minutes."

The radio crackled to life after a moment's pause.

"The Song of Seikilos." Campbell said, before swearing. "Sorry, not you. The bolt's stuck."

"The *what*?"

"Song of Seikilos." Campbell repeated. "Oldest complete musical composition on Earth. Found on a tombstone Seikilos left for his wife, circa 200BCE. Took Greek as an elective at McGill, learned it there. Listen."

She sang, and recited an English translation.

"Fitting epitaph for Earth?"

Robinson looked out toward the array, and actually smiled.

"Fitting enough for MacKenzie Campbell, PhD." She turned on the sound recorder. "One more time, luv. For posterity."

The mike was cheap and the radio, warbly. But it was the most beautiful thing Robinson had ever heard.

"There." She said. "Ready. Just need to push the button in...two minutes seventeen seconds. How are you doing?"

"All set up here. Going to sign off now. You need to focus. Need to...get the signal out. How long?"

Something was wrong.

"Campbell?"

"How long?!"

Glance at the timer.

"One minute."

Quiet hum, then:

"Too hot out here. Send out the Song of Seikilos. Make my Greek semester count for something."

MacKenzie, what—"

The radio squealed, so hard Robinson had to kill it. Ten seconds later, back on. But no matter how hard she called, only static hum would answer.

What in the – what had – Had she dropped her radio? No. That wasn't it. Robinson knew it wasn't. Campbell was...

She turned to the monitor. Silently, she counted down the last countdown.

"Go on, MacKenzie." Robinson muttered, before clicking the button.

There.

MacKenzie Campbell's last wish.

Charlotte Robinson sat back in her chair, and watched the world end.

After the terrible ghastly noise, an entire biosphere igniting in a paroxysm of cosmic rays, there was a terrible ghastly silence. The Earth fell quiet, never to speak again, except for the soft susurrations of water on rock. But the Sun, once every 28 days, sang into the heavens. An endless verse, repeated over and over, a testament to the first star in the Milky Way to nourish life.

Hóson zêis phaínou
mēdén hólōs sy lypoû
pros olígon estí to zên
to télos ho chrónos apaiteî.

> While you live, shine
> have no grief at all
> life exists only for a short while
> and time demands an end.

"Earth Epitaph" originally appeared in *Triangulation: Dark Skies*,
on 13 July 2019

About the author

A franco-californien armed with a wok and a word processor, R. Jean Mathieu has hauled sail, served tea, hung beef, sold cell phones, and once even used his own coat as a zip-line sixteen stories above the streets of Hong Kong. He writes every flavor of fiction under a variety of noms de plume. He and his wife, Melissa, keep a good table when not writing side-by-side or chasing trains to the next adventure. You can find Mathieu's stories in *Triangulation: Dark Skies, Solarpunk Winters*, and on Amazon. The man himself writes at RjeanMathieu.com.

L'Appel du Vide

Rajiv Moté

On Friday morning, the ambient heaviness in his boss's tiny office threatened to bend Isaac double, and his ears ached from the pressure in the air. The dread hadn't started with his boss's unexpected meeting request, but coalesced around it, wrapping the 15-minute block on his calendar in layers of doubt and worry until it shone like a fat, anxious pearl. It had been gathering over weeks. Office doors that usually stayed open were shut. Hallways and corners sheltered low, furtive conversations; Isaac felt like he was interrupting conspiracies every time he walked to the restroom. The very air resisted movement, its weight dragging down shoulders and gazes. It felt like the air before a storm cracks open the sky.

His boss, from across the desk, began by telling him what Isaac already knew.

"As you know…"

A disappointing Q2. A gloomy forecast for Q3. Streamlining. Tightening belts. Pivoting. Reorganizing. Isaac waited as each term in the well-rehearsed speech pulled him in, spiraling closer to the actual point.

"We have to let you go."

There. The dice showed their pips. The curtain pulled back. With the word "go," Isaac was unmoored.

First, figuratively, and then, a heartbeat later, literally. His boss was still talking while Isaac floated inches above his seat. He panicked for a moment, losing the leverage that came with gravity. Putting his feet back on the floor only pushed him up higher, until he was floating in the middle of the room. He began to tilt, and his arms and legs flailed for some kind of purchase. His boss's eyes held polite sympathy. He asked if Isaac had any questions. Isaac shook his head. In his flailing, he found he could change his orientation and even propel himself by pushing against the thickened air.

"Your belongings will be shipped to your home," his boss said, "so I'm going to ask that you leave the office now. This will be a difficult day here, and I'd appreciate if you helped minimize the distractions."

Experimentally, Isaac tucked his knees into his chest and flapped his arms.

"Do you need some help with the door?"

Isaac executed a slow, controlled roll in mid-air. As he faced the door, upside down, he took the opportunity to turn the knob and open it. "No," he said, keeping the emotion out of his voice. "I'm good." With a kick of his legs, he floated out among the cubicles.

"I'm out of a job," Isaac said, low enough for his own ears only, to confirm what his brain had only begun to process. He knew the danger of the ground falling out from under one's feet, the sensation of endlessly falling. It had happened a lot in the neighborhood where he grew up. Folks with no plan and no place to go, floating down the street or hovering over the corner, their arms and legs windmilling to stay upright. A strong wind could blow them away. Gone. Mama wouldn't have any of that from her boys. The moment he or his brother Ray started to rise an inch or two off the floor, she would pull them back down and stick their noses into a school book. Their mama said that the day their father walked out on them, he fell straight up into the air and probably burned himself to a crisp in the sun, good riddance to the man. Real men could be counted on to keep their feet on the ground.

Viewed from above, the rows of cubes looked small and orderly, the sense of sameness and pattern overwhelming people's attempts to stamp them with individual personalities. His colleagues—ex-colleagues— glanced up as he passed over them, but no more than glanced, as if the strain of lifting their eyes above their screens were too great in this heavy air. There was envy in some of those glances. 'Oh, this looks fun?' Isaac thought. 'See how fun it is when you can't stand up.'

He drifted over his own cube. On the desk were the computer and phone, which belonged to the company. A stack of papers he'd someday hoped to sort. A tiny dead cactus in a pot. Pens, notepads, a mug, a water bottle— all with the company logo. Relics. He was swimming over the sunken ruins of his last seven-odd years. There was also a framed picture of Tonya and the girls, Janae and Krista, ages seven and five. Tonya crouched behind the two girls, her hands around their shoulders. He called them his inspiration, the reason he was here. All three smiled wide, brilliant smiles, polished to a gleam by his employer-subsidized dental insurance.

"Good morning, ladies," he said, stretching his arm, reaching for the picture. All three beamed back. "I've got news. It's... not so good." Their big brown eyes were full of expectation. "But it'll wait."

Reaching far enough to strain his shoulder, he grasped the picture and traced the simulated grain of the fake wood frame with his fingertips. It was the only thing he managed to grab, but it was all he needed to take with him. He knew there were things down in the drawers too, but they were mostly what he put there without any intention of retrieving. Vendor swag, business cards, the employee handbook. He didn't need any of it anymore. He had never needed it. It was strange—all those hours here, and so little to mark his time.

"Hey man," Andre called to him on the way back from filling his coffee mug. "Moving up, I see."

"Yeah," Isaac said. "But not here."

Andre nodded, his expression becoming interested. "So it's begun, huh?" Andre had his ear to the company grapevine, and had guessed the reason behind the change in atmosphere. He called himself the Weatherman, because he knew which way the wind would blow.

Isaac nodded back, treading air. "You were right." It was strange to look down on Andre, who was a head taller than him.

Andre sighed. "Okay. Well. I'm not going say sorry, I'm going to say congratulations. Onward and upward. Good luck with whatever's next. And keep in touch, all right? Wherever you land, keep me in mind. I'll bet this is not over yet."

"Will do. Best of luck, man." The thought of landing was bleak. It felt as unreachable as the junk in his desk drawer. With a kick, he propelled himself down a hallway and through the break room, toward the exit. He avoided conversation, 'to minimize the distraction on this difficult day,' but he smiled and waved to former colleagues as he passed above them. Somehow, the smiles came easily. The work, follow-ups, and replies he owed several of them just weren't his problem anymore. There were nice reasons to lose touch with the ground too, at least for a while. First love could do it. Winning a scholarship. Getting the kind of job that had a real future. Isaac knew guys who came back from time served and didn't touch the ground for weeks until the old drama of the neighborhood got its hooks back in. Maybe this was what freedom felt like. His thumb stroked the plastic picture frame. Maybe this was how his father felt when he disappeared into the sky.

He realized what he must look like, floating to the lobby doors, smiling like a fool. He put on a serious expression, the expression of a man who understood the gravity of his situation and was carefully considering his next move. But his feet didn't quite touch the floor the way a man's did when he was carrying around serious thoughts. He was literally buoyant.

Not trusting the physics of weightlessness in an elevator, he took the stairs down the 14 floors to the lobby. He drifted on his belly down the stairwell, like a skydiver before the parachute opens. With nobody watching, he allowed himself a laugh. He added some flourishes, rotating his body like a drill, corkscrewing down the spiral. In the privacy of the stairwell, he felt more like a superhero than a man who had just lost the means to support his family. Then he had an idea—a crazy one—and he reversed direction. With a kick off the railing, he rose, up past the 14th floor, up to the 25th, where he touched the carpet only long enough to open the door to the rooftop deck.

It was June, and the lawn chairs and enormous shade umbrellas were out. People on their breaks, enjoying the sun and the view, turned when Isaac floated out onto the deck. "Well good for you," a woman said to him, and a young guy gave him a thumbs up. Maybe they thought he'd fallen in love. He hovered just above the high concrete railing and looked down. The wind was strong up here, but he wasn't completely unanchored. The smiling family in the picture frame he held kept him from getting too carried away. Below, the cabs, buses, and trucks on Jackson Boulevard jockeyed for position among the lanes, and people walked along the sidewalks, jaywalking when the lights turned red. There was a hum below that Isaac always liked.

It had been a dream of Isaac's to work downtown, amidst that bustle. That's what he had grown up thinking success looked like. Success was a destination, and he'd made it, against the odds. He'd done what was needed. The next pieces of his life had fallen into place more easily than he could believe. He'd earned promotions, gotten married, had kids, and even bought a house in a nice neighborhood.

But he was embarrassed to realize he hadn't given much thought to what made up the hours of daily life leading to that success. What occupied those hours was... hard to describe. He had a vague, jumbled impression of email, to-do lists, meetings, reports, whiteboards, spreadsheets, jargon, and coffee. It was a mire of busyness that spanned more than ten years and three companies, and every day he sank deeper. He didn't want to be ungrateful, but he'd lost track of the 'why.' His daughter Janae once asked him what his work was for, and he realized he didn't even know anymore.

Isaac glanced down at the framed photograph in his hands, and took a deep breath. It was heavier than it should have been, for wood-colored plastic. Soon, he'd have to deal with what would be next. He'd have to sell himself. The thought was heavier than the frame. But it didn't have to be right now. Not just this moment. Surely he'd earned a little fun on the way back down. He pushed against the air, moving out over Jackson Boulevard, 25 floors below. Slowly, like a bead sinking in honey, he descended. He gave a few kicks to make sure he could regain height, but once he was satisfied, he allowed gravity to exert its weakened pull and just enjoyed the sensation of floating.

He'd explored downtown longer than the decade he worked here, but he'd never seen it like this. In the corners outside windows he saw big spiders in their webs, anchored against the wind. He passed pigeons roosting on ledges, and even a falcon, considering which of the pigeons to murder. He sank past windows of offices and conference rooms, and waved on the way down. Some waved back. Others did their best to ignore him.

"Isaac!" called a voice. "Hey, man, come down!"

Ten floors below, on the sidewalk outside his ex-building's main lobby, Andre was calling up to him.

Isaac aimed himself and scooped at the air to descend faster. He stopped just short of the ground, hovering at eye level with Andre. He didn't let his feet touch down, for fear that he wouldn't rise again.

"They got me right after you," Andre said. "My boss didn't even put anything on the calendar. Complete drive-by. I hate being right all the time."

"Well, you're the Weatherman. I'm sorry. Or congratulations, if that's how you feel. So it's a bloodbath in there?" Isaac tried to sound sympathetic. Andre's feet were firmly on the ground.

"Yeah. I've heard of half a dozen, personally, but it's happening all through the company. I'm getting texts every fifteen minutes."

"So, are you going to... take some time?" Isaac liked Andre, but he didn't want to get pulled into the drama when he could be soaring among the buildings, examining mouldings and facades, and seeing everything from a new perspective. He'd earned this time to float free from the needs and expectations of others.

"That's why I called you down. I was talking to Samir, and it turns out he has some connections through a cousin. How would you like to work for our top competitor?" Andre bounced his eyebrows like he'd said something delightful and wicked.

Isaac dropped a couple of inches before he caught himself. "Doing what?"

"The same thing! Only for about $10K more, is what I'm hearing. Samir says he'll put in a word for both of us, but we have to move fast. Like you said, it was a bloodbath. We'll have competition."

Isaac felt gravity like a heavy cable reeling him back to earth. The picture frame in his hands was a lead weight. He kicked and waved his arms against the pull. It was all he could do to stay aloft.

"I get it, man," Andre said. "You just got kicked in the junk by a place you gave—what—five years? Take some time. Give yourself a start date a couple of weeks out. But don't give up on your passion because you got knocked down. You can't pass this up."

"Seven years." Isaac's toes brushed the concrete. Ten thousand dollars more. For whatever it was he did.

Their CEO had had a pep talk. 'If you're not passionate about what you do,' he'd say, 'then why are you even here?' Isaac didn't dare admit that in almost 12 years of professional life, he hadn't found a passion. But he could navigate an office, speak the jargon, follow process, and do things that brought modest, but not insignificant, increases to his paycheck every year. Tonya, Janae, and Krista smiled up at him from the picture in his hands. Maybe he had a passion for providing for his family. Taking Samir's job was the sensible thing to do. The safe thing. It was an unexpected lifeline in a sea of doubt. He ought to be grateful. It wasn't as if he had any other plan.

But the sky above, between the tall buildings, was the watercolor blue of early summer. He might never see it from up high again.

"I'm going to pass."

The words just came out, and before he could take them back, he felt a slack in the invisible cable tethering him. He pushed, and reclaimed a couple of inches of altitude. "I don't want to do this anymore." He was a head above Andre now. He caught a breeze.

"But what will you do, then?"

Isaac tried to think of an answer that sounded legitimate and responsible. Something that would describe a respectable place for him in the world as a contributor to his family, a provider for his kids. Something that wouldn't reveal just how much he was adrift. You can take the kid out of the 'hood...

"I have no idea," he finally said. More slack. Andre craned his neck to look up at him. "But I can't go back down there..."

Isaac rose like a party balloon with a cut string. As Andre became small and indistinguishable from the rest of the working crowd downtown, Isaac rode the wind, banking between buildings and circling landmarks laid out below him. At this height, the noise of the city was drowned out by the rush of air past his ears. Nobody could touch him here. Nobody could reach him. City blocks become patterns of multicolored geometry. Downtown became a cluster of tall buildings in a much larger city that hugged the lake, sprawling north, south, and west. And beyond it lay green, brown, and yellow rectangles of farms and prairie, crossed by ribbons of road and river, winding beyond sight even from this vantage. The world was vast. The world was very small.

Isaac shivered as he rose straight through a cumulus cloud. Breaking through to the top, he paused, momentarily blinded by the dazzling rainbow of diffracted sunlight, so bright the very air seemed to shine. Fluffy white islands drifted in the blue sky. He floated above a moderate-sized hill among dramatic cloud mountains, towers, and valleys, all shining white and pristine. The air was cold, but invigorating. He felt it entering and exiting his lungs, and his every sense felt sharp and alive.

Something whooshed past him with a cry of "Cannonball!" Isaac was horrified to see a person-shaped hole in the clouds beneath him. He let himself drop near the edge of the hole and peered down. Whoever had fallen was coming back up. He saw the red top of a knit winter hat rising toward him, with arms and legs below moving in a butterfly stroke. A shaggy-haired guy in a ski vest burst through the hole and let out a whoop.

"More like a belly flop, huh?" the man said as he rose alongside a fluffy plume of cloud.

Now that Isaac looked, he saw more people among the cumulus formations. Another man, this one in a suit and tie flapping in the wind, leaped from the top of the plume, executing a swan dive into the cloud. Others swam in and out of the cottony fluff, or snoozed in the sunlight. One was drifting on her back, reading a hardcover book. The realization jolted Isaac like a Monday alarm at 5 A.M. This was a thing. People lived like this. He didn't know whether to be astounded or furious.

Well he was here now. Isaac pushed off in pursuit of the shaggy man, spiraling up the plume. "Hey!" he called. "Hi!"

Shaggy paused, treading air for Isaac to catch up. "How's it going?" he called back.

"I had no idea about all this," Isaac said. "Is it... Is it always like this?"

Shaggy laughed. "New, huh?"

"I was laid off this morning."

Shaggy grinned with genuine enthusiasm. "Congratulations! Nice to be free, isn't it?"

Free? Isaac's eyes darted around the shining landscape as he was seized by the wild terror that he would see his father here, kicking back on a cloud. He kicked to regain some height. "It's something, alright."

Shaggy, whose name was actually Greg, introduced him to some of the other plume-divers. Most were regulars, and knew each other. They had a friendly competition going. Greg explained that to get any real speed, you needed to think of something that attached you 'to the world down there.' Obligations. Responsibilities. Something that really pulled at you. You dove, and at the last moment, you released it. And back up you went. "You want to try?"

The sun was just above the cloud line in the west. He'd have to go home soon. Go home and tell his family what had happened, and what he meant to do about it.

"Why not?" Isaac said.

He hovered above the tip of the plume and then raised the picture of Tonya, Janae, and Krista to his eyes. He said their names. He felt a tug somewhere in his gut. And then, before he could decide how to dive, he dropped like a stone. Isaac screamed. He heard a thin shout from above, nearly drowned out by the wind. "Just let go!"

No. His fingers clamped down on the plastic picture frame as he plummeted. 'No way in hell,' he thought. He wasn't like any of those people up playing in the clouds, privileged, without responsibilities, without a care in the world. He wasn't like those people in his old neighborhood, weighed down but still drifting. And he wasn't like his father. He had something besides himself to live and work for. He had a family. Something he'd die for.

'A fat lot of good that'll do us,' Tonya would have said. He looked down at the picture. The girls were still smiling, but Tonya was looking right at him, arching one eyebrow the way she did when she was done tolerating nonsense. Sometimes she used that eyebrow when telling him what he already knew—but she decided he needed to hear again. Things like 'If you don't want to be your father, then make a different choice. Be there for us. Be there for you.'

Isaac's fall slowed. She was right, of course. It wasn't his family weighing him down. He'd chosen what kind of man he wanted to be long ago. But that choice had gotten tangled up in the other things he thought he had to do. The mire that had slowly sucked him lower for years. Well, he was out of the mire now. Cut loose. So what next?

He realized he was no longer falling. The world was laid out before him, but the faces of Janae and Krista in the frame held his eyes. They were older now than when the photograph was taken, and even in Krista he saw glimmers of the women they'd become. They were more confident than he had been at that age. They laughed easier. They didn't live in fear of disappointing a parent who was embittered by loss, who never stopped working and never failed to remind her kids it was all for them. His kids were different. And he was different from his parents, either one.

He began to rise again. He rose, faster, and faster still. He wanted to fly. He needed to. He broke through the cloud plume and zoomed past Greg and the divers. He wasn't slowing down. At a certain height, rising became indistinguishable from falling. The air turned cold, thin, and weightless. The further he rose from the Earth, the less pull it exerted. Already the curve of the western horizon glowed crimson as the speck where he lived and once worked, far below, passed into the shadow of early evening.

The unobstructed night sky yawned above. What had started as black with a few pinpricks of light became a luminous river of heavenly bodies, from dust to planets, all reflecting the starshine. At the very precipice of the celestial chasm, everything seemed to fall away but what he chose to hold on to, like the picture frame that tethered him to a home in a nice neighborhood far below. Isaac stopped to take it all in. The emptiness had a pull of its own. All that space, never to be filled. He could imagine surrendering to the illuminated infinity, as easy as falling. It was thrilling in the way looking out over any beckoning abyss thrilled, as long as you trusted your anchor.

Isaac stretched his arms and legs wide, as if to embrace it all. He felt the cracks and pops as he stretched his neck and arched his back. His heart pounded. Blood roared in his ears. Nerves fired and flared like the stars themselves. He filled a portion of that vast emptiness with himself. His entire body shook with the sweet, savage joy of coming alive.

"L'Appel du Vide" originally appeared in *Metaphorosis,* on 22 March 2019

About the author

Rajiv Moté is a writer living in Chicago with his wife, daughter, and puppy. His stories make appearances in *Cast of Wonders, Diabolical Plots, Metaphorosis, McSweeney's Internet Tendency, Truancy*, and others, and he has served as a slush-reading Badger for Shimmer. During the day, he gathers source material by masquerading as a software engineering manager. He scrapes off excess words on Twitter at @RajivMote, and occasionally realizes he should put some effort into rajivmote.com.

Copyright

Anthology © 2020 Metaphorosis Publishing

Cover art by vegan artist Bonnie Leeman
bonniemarieleeman.daportfolio.com

"The Lonely King" © 2019, Gunnar De Winter
"Growing Resistance" © 2019, Juliet Kemp
"Rooks on Sundays" © 2019, Jack Neel Waddell
"The Trader" © 2019, Damien Krsteski
"The Soul Farmer's Daughters" © 2019, Kyle Kirrin
"Crying in Public" © 2019, Madi Giovina
"The Propagator" © 2019, Simone Kern
"A Bear, or a Spider, or an Elephant" © 2019, Edward
    Ashton
"The Silence of Mother" © 2019, Gerald Warfield
"The Color of My Home is Red Like an Apple" © 2019,
    Evan Marcroft
"There is a City, He Told Me" © 2019, Evan James
    Sheldon
"As An Absence" © 2019, Joanna Michal Hoyt

<u>First appearance</u>

All stories first appeared in *Metaphorosis,* except

"Growing Resistance" first appeared in *Translunar Travelers Lounge.*

"The Trader" first appeared in *Score – an SFF symphony.*

"Crying in Public" first appeared in *super / natural: art and fiction for the future.*

"The Silence of Mother" first appeared in *Score – an SFF symphony.*

"As An Absence" first appeared in *New Orbit.*

"The Shapeshifter Unraveled" first appeared in *Daily Science Fiction.*

"Earth Epitaph" first appeared in *Triangulation: Dark Skies.*

Metaphorosis Publishing

Metaphorosis offers beautifully written science fiction and fantasy. Our imprints include:

Metaphorosis Magazine

Plant Based Press

Verdage

Help keep Metaphorosis running at
Patreon.com/metaphorosis

See more about some of our books on the following pages.

Metaphorosis
a magazine of speculative fiction

Metaphorosis is an online speculative fiction magazine dedicated to quality writing. We publish an original story every week, along with author bios, interviews, and notes on story origins. Come and see us online at magazine.Metaphorosis.com

You can also find us at:
Twitter: @MetaphorosisMag, @MetaphorosisRev, @Metaphorosis
Facebook: www.facebook.com/metaphorosis

We publish monthly print and e-book issues, as well as yearly Best of and Complete anthologies.

**Metaphorosis:
Best of 2019**

The best science fiction and fantasy stories from *Metaphorosis* magazine's fourth year.

Metaphorosis 2019

All the stories from *Metaphorosis* magazine's fourth year. Fifty-two great SFF stories.

Metaphorosis:
Best of 2018

The best science fiction
and fantasy stories from
Metaphorosis magazine's
third year.

Metaphorosis 2018

All the stories from
Metaphorosis magazine's
third year. Fifty-two great
SFF stories.

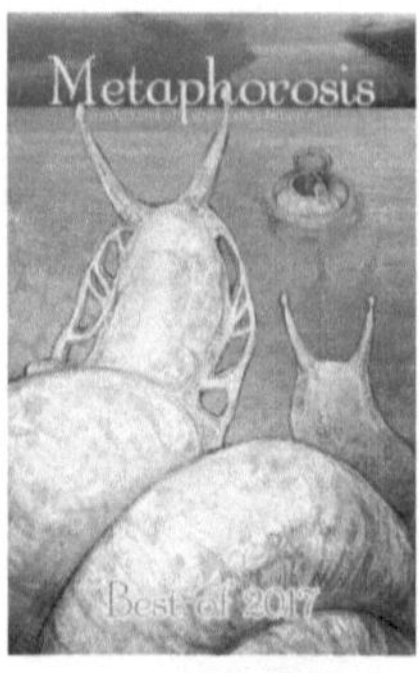

Metaphorosis:
Best of 2017

The best science fiction
and fantasy stories from
Metaphorosis magazine's
second year.

Metaphorosis 2017

All the stories from
Metaphorosis magazine's
third year. Fifty-three
great SFF stories.

Metaphorosis:
Best of 2016

The best science fiction
and fantasy stories from
Metaphorosis magazine's
first year.

Metaphorosis 2016

Almost all the stories from
Metaphorosis magazine's
first year.

Plant Based Press

Vegan-friendly science fiction and fantasy, including an annual anthology of the year's best SFF stories.

Best Vegan SFF of 2019

The best vegan science fiction and fantasy stories of 2019!

Best Vegan SFF of 2018

The best vegan science fiction and fantasy stories of 2018!

Best Vegan SFF
of 2017

The best vegan science fiction and fantasy stories of 2017!

Best Vegan SFF
of 2016

The best vegan science fiction and fantasy stories of 2016!

Susurrus

A darkly romantic story of magic, love, and suffering.

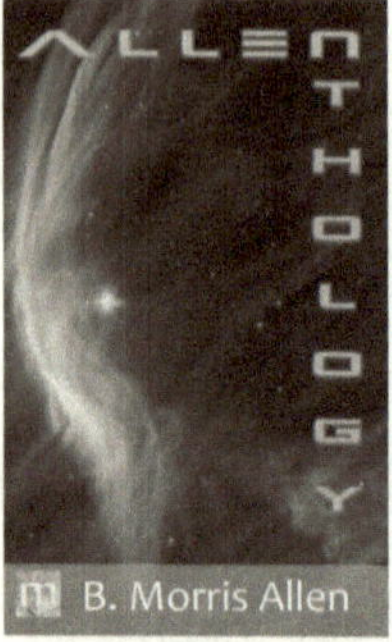

Allenthology:
Volume I

A quarter century of SFF, including the full contents of the collections *Tocsin, Start with Stones,* and *Metaphorosis.*

Verdage

Science fiction and fantasy books for writers – full of great stories, but with an additional focus on the craft of speculative fiction writing.

Score

an SFF symphony

What if stories were written like music? *Score* is an anthology of varied stories arranged to follow an emotional score from the heights of joy to the depths of despair – but always with a little hope shining through.

Reading 5X5

Five stories, five times

Twenty-five SFF authors, five base stories, five versions of each – see how different writers take on the same material, with stories in contemporary and high fantasy, soft and hard SF, and a mysterious 'other' category.

Reading 5X5

Writers' Edition

All the stories from the regular, readers' edition, plus two extra stories, the story seed, and authors' notes on writing. Over 100 pages of additional material specifically aimed at writers.

www.ingramcontent.com/pod-product-compliance
Lightning Source LLC
Chambersburg PA
CBHW050253110726
47898CB00007B/2392